THE CHOICE

This fictionalised account of All-Ireland-winner Philly McMahon's life is based on his multi-award-winning memoir for adults, *The Choice*. Winner of the Bord Gáis Energy Irish Sports Book of the Year and the Éir Sports Book of the Year, the memoir was widely acclaimed and a huge bestseller in Ireland. Now, this moving and inspirational book, written again with Niall Kelly, will reach a whole new generation of readers, in a coming-of-age story about family, fate and the decisions that shape our lives.

Philly McMahon won eight All-Irelands with the Dublin football team before retiring at the end of 2021. Philly is also a performance coach with Bohemians, an entrepreneur and a social activist. Since losing his brother, John, in 2012, Philly has become an outspoken advocate for addiction and mental health initiatives and is passionate about intervention for young people. **Niall Kelly** is a journalist and Deputy Editor of The42.ie. Niall worked with Philly on his award-winning and best-selling memoir for adults and with Barry Geraghty on *True Colours*, which won the Telegraph Sports Awards International Autobiography of the Year. This is his first work of fiction.

THE CHOICE

FOR YOUNG READERS

PHILLY McMAHON
WITH NIALL KELLY

GILL BOOKS

Gill Books
Hume Avenue
Park West
Dublin 12
www.gillbooks.ie

Gill Books is an imprint of M.H. Gill and Co.

© Philly McMahon 2022

9780717192861

Designed by Bartek Janczak
Edited by Emma Dunne
Proofread by Esther Ní Dhonnacha
Printed and bound by Clays Ltd, Suffolk
This book is typeset in 12 on 17pt, Adobe
Garamond Pro.

5 4 3 2 1

For Mam and Dad, for all you've done for us
For Sarah and Leannain, for all we'll do together

I engraved me name on the pillars of the arch
So that when I left I'd always leave me mark.
Everything I am, I owe to you.
– Gemma Dunleavy, 'Up De Flats'

1

got my head out of the way just in time. The skin of his knuckles brushed the side of my cheek, like your mam might do if you had a bit of dirt on your face, and missed.

I didn't want a fight. But I didn't have much of a choice now. So I took a step towards him and took a swing back.

A spark of electricity shot through the crowd. There must have been forty lads there watching us, fencing us in in a circle so that even if we wanted to leg it we couldn't, and once they saw those first punches, they knew they were going to get what they came for. Game on.

Eddie Moran bounced around on his feet like a boxer, shouting at me, shouting at himself, trying to figure out his next move. And for what?

Eddie Moran was from Shangan. I was from Sillogue. He slagged my ma. I slagged his da.

And now we had to fight.

The school yard wasn't the place for it, and even if, earlier in the day, the two of us had wanted to go back inside to the classroom, sit down and forget about it, we weren't allowed to. The fuse had been lit, and the news had spread like wildfire, desk to desk.

'Scrap up at the Monos after school. Eddie and Philly. Pass it on.'

'Eddie's going to batter him. Pass it on.'

'Philly's da's in the 'RA. Pass it on.'

When there was a fight, the best spot to watch it from was on top of one of the Monos, these two long rows of tall, round stones and concrete cubes of different shapes and sizes. They were supposed to be art, I think, but for us, they were a ready-made boxing ring. If you were up on top, you had a great spot to see everything, and there was much less risk of being dragged into the middle of it.

Because even though these things started as a one-on-one, it didn't take much for them to end up as something bigger. It was a bit stupid that you had to be Sillogue or Balcurris or Balbutcher or Shangan because that was where you lived and that was who you hung around with. Stupid that lads who lived two minutes around the corner from each other and went to school together were told they hated each other.

At the end of the day, we were all from Ballymun, and Ballymun was bigger than everywhere.

But that was just the way it was.

Now, Eddie Moran was moving, shaping, taking two steps closer to me and then one step back, just to see how I'd react. I caught Kev's eye as we went around in a circle again. Kev had his jumper off, his tie off and the sleeves of his shirt rolled up around his elbows. He nodded when he saw me look over at him, encouraging me with his eyes. He wouldn't jump in unless one of the Shangan lads jumped in. Or unless things were getting bad and Eddie needed to be dragged off me. He was my best friend, but Kev didn't want to be there either.

A driver beeped his car horn at us as he pulled away from the traffic lights, but nobody paid any attention. It would take more than a few beeps to break up a scrap. The next time Eddie came at me, I went for a low kick to try to catch him around the ankles and knock him off balance. I knew I wasn't close enough to hit him, but I had to at least look like I was trying and not playing for a draw.

If this turned into a proper scrap and I got my jumper ripped, I'd have to go home and explain it. If my mam didn't have time to fix it, I'd have to wear it in to school the next day still ripped, or I'd have to wear a different jumper instead. Either way, it sounded like an easy ticket to another detention once Mr McEvoy spotted me. Or worse again, I could get hurt and miss training.

So, yeah, there was a lot at stake for a fight that I really didn't want to be in.

But as I said, I didn't have a choice. Because in Ballymun, the only thing worse than losing a fight was running away from one. You'd only have a black eye for a couple of weeks, but you'd have your reputation forever.

'Are yous fighting or what? Come on!' A voice I didn't recognise shouted in at us, and the frustration spread like a ripple.

'Stop just dancing around,' someone else shouted. 'One of you do something.'

And then the chanting started, one or two voices by themselves at first: 'Fight. Fight. Fight.'

Until more joined in and then everyone was at it: 'FIGHT. FIGHT. FIGHT.'

A sudden shove in my back shot me forward into the middle of the circle and I stumbled, off balance, right into Eddie's fist. He caught me square underneath my right eye, right on the bone. The crack of his punch sounded like it had come from somewhere very far away, but my whole face felt like it had burst into flames. I fell backwards, managing to stay on my feet. I took my hand away from my face and, through my one open eye, quickly checked it for blood. Nothing. Yet.

The world flipped upside down and I landed with a thump, my back slamming into the stony earth. Eddie had sensed his moment and wrestled me to the ground. I did my best to cover up, waiting for him to start swinging wildly, but instead, he flipped me so I was lying face down. With one knee in the middle of my back, and one knee on my neck, he pressed.

All he wanted was to hear me say that I quit. To say that he had won. That was my only way out of this now.

There was shouting and cheering, and it was getting louder. They were getting what they wanted. Eddie put more weight into his knee, pressing like he'd happily snap my neck if I didn't give up first. The ground was cool, but the pebbles were embedding themselves into the side of my face. It was getting hard to breathe, to get the air into my lungs, when another person was putting every last bit of effort into keeping me down. I started feeling dizzy, like I was going to pass out.

'All right, I quit. I quit.' I had no choice, but the words hadn't left my lips yet when everything lifted. The pain shooting through my neck stopped. I could breathe.

'What the –?' Eddie cried out, as surprised as anyone. 'Get your hands off me!'

I rolled over before I was trampled on, expecting all hell to break loose, when a big hand grabbed my collar and dragged me back onto my feet.

It was John.

—

'You didn't need to hop in for me,' I argued as we walked back towards home. 'I could have got him myself.'

'That's not what it looked like,' John said, my school-bag hanging on his shoulder. 'And that's not much of a thank you, is it?'

'Yeah, but now I'm going to be the lad whose big brother hops in for him.'

John laughed. 'And what? Is that a bad thing? I'd have loved to have a big brother hopping in for me. No harm having lads think that I'll come around and batter them if they touch you. It might make them leave you alone. Anyway,' he said, giving me a little dig in the arm, 'you'd have been picking bits of gravel out of your teeth for a week if I hadn't shown up.'

'It wasn't that bad, shut up,' I said. And then, eventually, 'Thanks for getting him off me, though. I thought he was going to break my neck.'

John smelled like blood – not human blood, animal blood. He worked up in the Meat Packers, a big factory out near the airport. He had worked there for three years, maybe four. He started off when he was 16, doing one shift a week; he went out on his lunch break one day to collect his Junior Cert results and he never went back to school again. It was his job to pick up the slabs of raw meat from the butchers' counter, where they'd been hacking them apart, and carry them over to the packaging counter so they could be boxed up and sent out to the shops. He had to wear plastic overalls and special gloves so the meat didn't get contaminated, but his clothes still stank every day when he came in the door. He wouldn't even need to say hi or call out that he was home: you'd smell him before you'd see him.

'How come you're home so early anyway?' I asked him. I didn't know what time it was – around four o'clock, maybe – but John was never back from work before six, except maybe sometimes on Fridays.

He started walking a bit more slowly, as though he needed to concentrate for a second so he could remember. 'Ah yeah,' he said, when he finally answered me. 'I got a half-day to go around breaking up fights. Neighbourhood watch, y'know?'

'Stop lying. Why aren't you still in work?'

We had slowed down to a complete stop now.

'All right. Just don't tell Mam and Dad. I'm after getting sacked.'

'What? For what?'

'For nothing. Honestly, I didn't do anything wrong.' He was more angry than upset, which made me believe him. 'You know what they're like up there – they just find a reason. It's a different story if you're working on the machines, but they can get new lads in for the floor easy, and then they pay them less too.'

'Did they give you a reason?'

He pulled a piece of paper out of his pocket. 'Yeah, they said I'd been on an official warning for being late, and then I was late again. But' – he took a look at the page in his hand before crumpling it back up – 'I wasn't even late on most of those days. It's just that the clock-in machine doesn't always be working.'

'Did Aaron get sacked too?'

Aaron was John's best friend and nearly like another big brother to me. Everywhere one of them went, the other was there too. They were always together, a bit like me and Kev.

'Nah, Aaron's grand. His supervisor seems all right – he has a different one than I do. Than I did,' he said, correcting himself.

'How are they able to just sack you like that anyway?' I asked as we walked across the field. 'I thought there'd have to be a law or something.'

But John didn't say anything until we stopped at the bottom of the stairwell. The blocks of flats stood in a line, side by side like concrete soldiers following the curve of the road. This had been our home for the last 13 years, in the four-storeys on Sillogue Avenue, but Ballymun came in all shapes and sizes. There were the eight-storeys, like the blocks around the corner where our family lived until I was born and they needed a bigger flat for a fifth child, and then there were the Towers – seven blocks of flats, each one fifteen storeys high, soaring over us all.

'Anyway, I won't say anything about the fight to Mam and Dad, and you say nothing about the job,' John said to me as we started up the stairs to the first floor.

It wouldn't take a detective to figure out about the fight. The lump under my eye was already sore to touch, and I knew there'd be a nasty-looking bruise. I wanted to get inside so I could have a proper look at it in the mirror. 'You're not going to tell them?'

'No, they'll only be worrying,' he said as he took my schoolbag off his shoulder and handed it back to me. 'One of the lads thinks he'll be able to sort me out with a new job soon, so I'll tell them the full story once I've got everything sorted, and then there'll be nothing to worry about.

'Anyway,' he said, pushing open the front door to let me go in ahead of him, 'say nothing.'

2

Kellie's schoolbag was already sitting in the hall inside the front door, and from the kitchen, I could hear the clang of pots and pans as my sister started to get the dinner ready. Mam and Dad wouldn't be in from work for a while yet.

I pushed her bag aside with the toe of my shoe and dropped mine beside it. Her bag was as light as a feather, and without even looking, I knew there was nothing in it except her sketch-pads and pens and pencils.

'Transition Year,' she'd said when I had asked her

why she only ever seemed to have her art supplies with her. 'No books, no homework.'

The maths book and the history book in my bag felt heavy by comparison. At least I had remembered to bring them home this time, even if I had no plans to look at them.

John turned straight in to our bedroom while I poked my head in to the kitchen to say hi to Kellie. The flat was quiet apart from whatever song she was humming to herself as she peeled potatoes and dropped them into a pan of water. I left her and went into the sitting room to lie down on the floor, underneath the window where the heat came up through the boards from the warm pipes below, and I didn't move again until Dad came home a little while later.

'Well, any stories for me?' he asked, his big frame filling his chair as he lowered himself into it. I hadn't even bothered to switch the television on, but the chair directly facing it was always Dad's spot, whether he was reading the paper or dozing off in front of the evening news.

'Nah, nothing really,' I said, turning my face slightly to the side as I sat up in the hope that he wouldn't spot my black eye. Dad had already changed out of his work clothes, but the cement dust from a day on the building site hadn't budged from the cracks and grooves of his hands.

The crispy smell of roast chicken filled the flat, and Mam followed it all the way into the kitchen when she came home. I didn't need to look at the time to know that it was ten past six. Egan's, the little hardware company where Mam worked, was a few minutes up the road. She ran the office, doing the phones and taking orders and checking the deliveries, and apart from on the bad days, she was always home at ten past six. She looked tired as she ran her hands through the top of my hair and collapsed next to Dad, giving him a kiss on the cheek as she sank into the couch.

As the youngest, it was my job to bring the knives and forks into the sitting room, but I waited until Kellie was taking the dinner out of the oven before I counted them out from the drawer. It was five tonight, but some nights it might be three or four if Mam or Dad were caught late in work or if I had training; some nights, it could even be six or seven if June or Lindy, our two older sisters, were there. They had their own flats down the road. Some nights, Kev might have dinner with us; some nights, Trish, his mam, would invite me to stay for dinner in theirs. You never knew. That's why it was best to wait until the last minute for the knives and forks.

'What happened your eye, Philip?' Mam noticed it as she sat back down, ribbons of steam rising off the plate on her knee. 'Tell me that you got a bang playing football and that you weren't fighting. Is that from fighting?' she said, not even giving me the chance to answer her.

John got in ahead of me while I had a mouthful of chicken. 'You'd want to see the other lad, though – isn't that right, Philly?' he said, picking up a potato with his fork. He looked at Kellie apologetically as he put it down on my plate. 'They're gorgeous, Kellie, thanks. You know what I'm like with potatoes – I'm all right with two this evening. Philly needs the energy anyway. He's the athlete in this family.'

'How'd you know what the other lad looked like?' Dad wasn't interested in counting out spuds.

'What do you mean?' John said.

'You just said that we'd want to see what the lad Philly was fighting looked like afterwards. How would you know what he looked like? Were you not in work today?'

Dad didn't miss much. When you thought he wasn't really listening or paying attention, that was when he was at his most dangerous.

'I was working, yeah,' John said, his eyebrows lifting ever so slightly as he looked at me. Kellie was the only one to notice. She knew we were up to something.

John kept going. 'I just mean Philly told me all about it. He must have learned something from me after all,' he said and started humming the theme tune from the *Rocky* films, shadow-boxing into the middle of the room.

'Enough, John,' Mam said, batting away an imaginary left hook. 'Eat your dinner and stop messing. And Philip, no more fighting please.'

'I didn't start it,' I explained. 'I was only fighting back. I'm allowed fight back.'

Mam changed the subject quickly before we got into the ins and outs of who started what and of when it was okay to be getting into scraps. 'Are you all coming with me to the march tomorrow? Don't have me going on my own. The papers are going to be there, and Claire Mac is after hearing that RTÉ are sending down a camera as well.'

Dad snorted, loud enough so that we could all hear. Seven other families shared our block of flats, and the MacCarthys were one of them. They lived two floors up and Claire was one of Mam's best friends. Any time she called down, she always had a quiet bit of 'news' about someone we knew; Dad often said she was so good at making up stories, she should have been out making films in Hollywood.

'Ah, stop that, Phil, she's had a very hard year,' Mam said. 'But I know what you mean – I'll believe it when I see myself on the nine o'clock news. Anyway, we need to be getting as many people out as possible.'

'I'll be home to go anyway,' Dad said.

'Yeah, me too,' Kellie said. 'I've my sign nearly finished and all.'

She went in to her bedroom and came back with a big double sheet of white cardboard to show us. Around the edges she had drawn a coffin, a syringe and a very lifelike human skull with a few thin lines of cracks running through the top of it. Kellie had always loved anything arty. When I was little, I helped her to lay an old bedsheet over the sitting-room table so she could try to teach me how to paint; the first thing I did was knock over a big pot of red paint when I was dipping my brush in the water, and then I understood what the sheet was for.

'I just need to finish the letters,' she said, turning the sign to make sure that we all got a good look. Taking up most of the space in the middle, she'd used a pencil to trace the outline of the message PUSHERS = MURDERERS.

'What about you, Philip?' Mam asked.

'We've training tomorrow night, but if I'm back in time, I'll come up to wherever you are and meet you afterwards.'

I knew the route they would be taking. Drug dealing in Ballymun wasn't an open secret; it wasn't a secret at all. Everyone knew where the dealers lived, and if you didn't, the steady stream of people filing in and out of certain blocks of flats, oblivious to everything in the world except for one thing, knocking on the same few doors, would make it obvious.

Marches like this had been happening since the 1980s, since before I was born, and they were still happening. They were our only way to fight back.

'They don't care about us, Philip. They never cared,' Mam said one day when I asked why the guards didn't just arrest the dealers if everyone knew who they were and what they were doing. She sounded tired even explaining it to me. 'If you went out and robbed a few sweets from a shop in Drumcondra tomorrow, they'd be on this doorstep with handcuffs and a warrant before you even got home again. But this? Sure, this is just us killing our own. Chuck them all into the flats, let them figure it out for themselves – that's how they think. Out of sight and out of mind for them. They only care if they have to.'

There had been hundreds of people on the last march, people like Mam and Dad, with their banners and their signs and their chants. Some of them were holding candles, trying to make little shields around the flames with their hands to keep them lit as they walked along. Claire Mac had a photo frame that she hugged in to her chest. It was a picture of her son Wayne; he had died of an overdose last year. Me and Kellie stood outside the church for his funeral, there were that many people trying to get in, but Mam and Dad and John got seats inside.

And all of these people, they showed up outside the block where the drug dealer lived, their voices never stopping, demanding that he come outside and face them:

PUSHERS. PUSHERS. PUSHERS.

OUT. OUT. OUT.

WHAT DO WE WANT?

PUSHERS OUT.

WHEN DO WE WANT IT?

NOW.

He promised that night that he'd stop, that he'd change, and while the line of people going up and down the stairwell wasn't quite as long or as frequent any more, there was still a line, people coming from all over the city like tourists on their holidays, getting off the 13 bus, drawn to the same doors.

Even after everything, he was still only one dealer out of many.

'Would they not move your training to another night?' Mam asked.

'I dunno. We've a match on Saturday against St Christopher's so they probably can't change it.'

'John?' she said.

'I'm working tomorrow,' he said. 'There's a double delivery coming in so they've asked some of us to work a late shift. It's double pay so I said I'd do it.' He winked at me but Kellie spotted him again.

'The two of you are up to something,' she said, pointing at John. 'What's going on?'

John shot me a look as if it was my fault that she'd seen him, but there was no need for him to wink at me every time he told a lie about work. I hadn't forgotten, and anyway, my lips were zipped.

I'd no idea if his story about the double delivery and the late shifts was true, apart from the fact that he wasn't involved, or if he'd completely made it up on the spot. If it was a lie that he'd just thought up there and then, it was a good one – but why did he need to lie at all? What was he doing instead of going to the march? And whatever it was, why didn't he just say it?

Dad had picked up an apple pie for dessert on the way home as a treat. I didn't really feel like having any so John had my slice instead – 'swaps for the potato earlier' – and then afterwards, the two of us did the dishes together.

'Right, I'm going out for a while – see yis later,' he said as he threw the tea-towel back on to the draining board.

'I'm coming with you,' I said. If I tagged along now, he'd have to let me hang out with him and his friends for a while.

'Don't be too late,' Mam shouted after us as I ran out the door behind John. 'And I'm talking to both of you.'

3

Aaron pulled a can out of the plastic bag at his feet and tossed it in our direction as we sat down to join him and the rest of John's friends: Ciarán, Trev, Joey and Denise Flynn. John got his hand underneath it just before it hit the ground.

'What?' Aaron said, expecting John to say something to him. The music wasn't particularly loud but he reached over to turn it down a small bit anyway. 'It's only a can. It's not like he hasn't seen you drinking before.'

John shrugged his shoulders as he cracked it open

in one move using the same hand. It fizzed, the white foam shooting out over the top, and John quickly put his mouth over it before it could spill everywhere.

'What's the story anyway, Young Caffo?' Aaron said to me while John took his first swig and made that noise that people always seemed to make whenever they had a drink of beer. 'Hope you've your homework done if you're out here with us on a school night.' That was one of his favourite jokes.

John's friends called him Caffo rather than John or Johnno or just by our surname, Caffrey, so Aaron decided that he was going to call me Young Caffo. That became my nickname then from all of John's friends. They were the only ones who called me Young Caffo, nobody else, but I liked it.

John's friends were sound – this group of friends anyway. The four lads had all gone to school together and got out of school together when they were 16, except for Joey. He was the only one of them who stayed on to do his Leaving Cert. Denise was sitting next to Aaron, and she smiled over at me as we sat down. The Flynns lived in the flat next door to us, all girls: Denise, her two little sisters and their mam. All of the Flynns were like models, really tall with long blonde hair that ran half the way down their backs. Michelle, the youngest, was three days older than me. Kev never stopped talking about her. But then any time we saw her, he just stood there with his hands in his pockets and didn't really say much.

The sun had just started to disappear behind the flats but it was a dry evening, and the back field behind our block was full of life, with groups gathered in fours and fives or more, all doing the same thing: listening to music, drinking, smoking, talking, messing. You had to make your own fun in Ballymun. I loved when Dad brought me swimming up in the corpo pool, and there was a youth club up in the White Elephant, our community centre, but other than that, we were on our own. During the day, any patch of grass could be turned into a football pitch in a couple of seconds, but at night, sitting out in the field was the place to be.

I could see our flat from where we were sitting, the light on in Kellie's bedroom, the clothes that Mam had left out in the hope that they'd dry on the balcony. John sipped away at his can. When he was younger, he used to hang out around the corner outside the eight-storeys, but he was 19, nearly 20, now. He hadn't needed to hide the fact that he was having a few drinks for a couple of years.

Any of the nights I was with him, this was the group he hung around with. That suited me. Other nights, he'd be with some other lads that I didn't know that well – Daz Kearns and some of those lads, who were all a bit older. Me and Kev would kick the ball over towards them to try and see what they were up to, but as soon as John spotted us, he'd tell us to get lost.

Now, I stretched my legs out into the middle of the circle to get a bit more comfortable, careful not to knock over any of the cans. Aaron was in the middle of telling a story.

'Would you ever give it up about bleedin' Bob Marley?' Trev said, scrunching up a receipt from his pocket so he could throw it at Aaron and hit him in the head. 'You can't fancy a dead man.'

Aaron owned the boombox so Aaron picked the music, and Aaron loved Bob Marley. He only owned one album, though – the one that had 'One Love' on it, and the other song where he's saying don't worry – and so he played the same ten or eleven songs over and over again. Sometimes he'd give Trev or John a shot at the music and they'd put on the mad American rap that they were into, or Ciarán would try to get him to play some UB40. But, most nights, it was Bob Marley.

'If you shut up for a second and listen to me,' Aaron carried on, ignoring him, 'all I'm saying is that Trench Town, the place he grew up in, was full of gangs and guns and poor people –'

'Yeow, Bob Marley lived in the flats!' Ciarán shouted, looking up from the rollie he was carefully putting together in his lap.

'Shut up you too, ye dope, it was poorer than the flats. This is in Jamaica. Anyway, what I'm saying to you is that because of his life, because of where he grew up, he had something to say to people. He just had that music inside him and had to get it out.'

'And what have you got inside you?' Trev said. 'A bit of steak that you whipped from work?'

That got a laugh out of everyone, including Aaron. John brought home a few chops or a cut of beef from the factory over the years too. He said they'd have ended up in the bin otherwise.

'Bob Marley loved a spliff too,' Ciarán pointed out through the corner of his mouth, the finished joint between his lips.

'He did, yeah.' Aaron nodded. The wail of sirens put an end to the music lesson for a moment, and everyone craned their heads to see what it was and where it was going. It had got dark very quickly, and the blue lights lit us up for a second as an ambulance shot through the junction without stopping and sped on in the direction of the Towers.

Denise looked on up the road after it and blessed herself with a little sign of the cross. Any time I heard a siren, I hoped for a garda car rather than an ambulance. A garda car could mean anything – it could just be young fellas who'd jumped over some wall into somewhere that they weren't supposed to be. An ambulance was always bad news, though.

The sound moved off into the night, like the volume on the TV slowly being turned down, but it never faded to zero. It always stopped somewhere nearby before it got that far away. And it wouldn't be long until the next one.

I didn't notice the man who had joined the group until Joey gave me a push to move over and make space. The man sat down between Denise and Aaron but didn't say anything. He nodded his head a few times, like he was agreeing with whatever had just been said, except nobody had said anything. A song finished, and there was nothing but silence for a second until the drums kicked in and Bob Marley started singing again.

He was older, an adult, and I didn't recognise him. He was wearing a big dark duffel coat, even though it hadn't got cold yet, black jeans and a pair of white runners that looked like they were straight out of the box, never worn before. His black baseball cap was pulled down low so that his eyes could barely be seen, and underneath it, I could just about make out the shaved sides of his haircut.

Nobody spoke until he spoke. 'Any smokes, lads?'

Ciarán pulled the yellow pouch of tobacco back out from inside his jacket and offered it in his direction, but the man had already lost interest, and now he was staring straight at John.

'I haven't seen you around much lately,' he said.

John looked straight back at him, not blinking, not losing eye contact for a second, but didn't even acknowledge that the man had spoken. He didn't say a word.

'Are you thick? I'm talking to you,' the man barked, not caring who heard him, and I jumped a little. Beside me, Joey clicked the nails of his thumb and forefinger together nervously and then stopped. He didn't want to draw the man's attention to himself.

When John spoke, he was calm, like the entire situation – whatever it was – was all a big misunderstanding. But there was a hardness to his voice too, making it clear that he wasn't going to be pushed around. 'Amn't I here?' he said. 'Same as always.'

The man finally stopped staring at John and moved his eyes around the group, looking at each of us slowly. I looked down at my hands before he got to me. They were shaking, but not so much that anyone else would notice. I tried to count the clicks of Joey's nails but he stopped again by the time I got to three.

Then, as suddenly and unexpectedly as he had arrived, the man left. He stood up, zipped up his coat, and walked away. 'See yis later, lads.' He turned back, the streetlight catching one half of his face. 'Take care of yourselves.' Those last words were more of a threat than a blessing.

As soon as he was out of earshot, Aaron looked over at John, a frown of confusion on his face. 'What was that all about?'

When he answered, John looked at me as if I was the one who had asked the question. 'Ah, it's nothing, I dunno,' he said. His eyes shot to Aaron and then quickly back to me. 'Never seen the lad before in my life,' he said, but he didn't sound too sure.

And before anyone could press him any further, he looked over at me and flicked his head in the direction of home. 'Come on, you better go. Mam said not to be too late. If she's asking, tell her I'll be up in twenty minutes.'

I knew there was more to the story than he was letting on, and I wanted to stay to hear it, but John insisted. When I left, I left slowly, but they waited until they were sure I was gone. I turned to look back and saw them huddled together, all of them asking John their questions at the same time. I tried to pick out even one word of what was being said, but no matter how hard I tried, all I could hear was the night.

4

It started to rain again, little spits of drops, as I picked up the final five or six cones and jogged back towards the trees where we'd left the rest of our gear bags. Kev took the cones from me, put them into the bag he had in his hand and zipped it closed while Colm counted off the footballs to make sure they were all present and accounted for.

I could have kept training for another half an hour, another hour, if I was let, but everybody else had gone home and now we were the last three left in the park, gathering up the gear to bring it back to Colm's car.

The lads in school always wanted to ask us about Colm. They had questions. They wanted to hear a story. At least, all of the ones who were into GAA did. Sometimes, Colm would knock in to the classroom, stick his head around the door and ask the teacher if he could have a quick word with me and Kev. And everyone in the room would be watching us as we got up from our desks and went out to speak to him, wishing it was them who had been called outside. I loved that I was the one being picked. I loved that they were all a bit jealous.

Because as well as being the manager of the Ballymun Kickhams Under-14 Gaelic football team, Colm Doyle played for Dublin. He was a defender, like me, except he was one of the best defenders in the country. Whenever Dublin played, Colm was the one picked to mark the best forward on the other team. I'd watched him play loads of times on telly, and it was like he had a sixth sense, like he knew where the forward was going to go and what he was going to do before the forward even knew himself. A hard player but a fair player: that's what they always said about Colm in the commentary.

He opened the boot of his car so me and Kev could pack away the training gear. It was one of the nicest cars I'd even seen in real life: a sports car, ruby red, that had only two doors at the front and none at the back. The

Little Red Buzzer, we called it. Colm thought that was gas. He was 20 years older than us, but we always had a good laugh with him.

'See you at half twelve on Saturday, lads,' he said as he climbed into the front seat. We loved getting a lift home from Colm in the Buzzer, but Poppintree Park, where we trained and played our home matches, was only a five-minute walk home for us, and he was going in the opposite direction. He lived in Glasnevin, on the other side of the poshie wall.

I don't know who came up with the name but that was what everyone in Ballymun called it. The two areas were side by side, and before the wall, it was hard to know exactly where one ended and the other one started. That's why the wall was built, to mark out the boundary. It was because of the drugs, I presumed – as if to say this side of the wall has no drug problem and is a good place, but that other place, on the other side of the wall, you don't want to go there. That's a bad place.

It seemed silly to me. Colm was from Glasnevin and he wasn't a poshie, even though we'd been inside his house a couple of times and it was lovely, and it had a massive back garden. Loads of lads on our team were from Glasnevin as well, like Jimmy and Liam and Taz – it was nearly a 50/50 split, if you counted everyone up. They weren't really poshies either.

'Do you know who the ref is yet?' I asked Colm before he closed the door. He was annoyed that I'd even asked him.

'It doesn't matter who the ref is, Philly, you know that. You can't control that. You can't be worrying about stuff like that. The ref didn't kick the ball over the bar for them the last time, did he?'

'He might as well have,' Kev said, butting in.

We'd been waiting months for this game, since last season's league final when St Christopher's beat us by a point. There were loads of teams that we loved beating, but right now, St Christopher's were top of the list. We had both finished level on points at the end of last season, and there was a coin toss before the league final to decide where it would be played. They won the toss, which meant we had to play in their ground on the southside, and they had a huge crowd there supporting them, shouting and roaring at the ref for the entire game. Most of them had obviously never played football before because they seemed to think every tackle was a foul.

And then, just when the ref should have been blowing the whistle for full time and a draw and a replay back in Ballymun, where we'd make sure we had twice as many people there to watch, he gave them the softest free I'd ever seen. It was as if the Christopher's player had been blown over by a gust of wind. It could only have been a gust of wind, because there wasn't a single one of our players within two feet of him. We tried to talk to the ref, and when that didn't work, we tried to argue with him, but nothing was going to change his mind. They popped the ball over the bar, and the ref blew the final whistle before Martin, our goalkeeper, even had time to take the kickout.

Colm made us stay and watch while they went up to collect their medals and their trophy. I could still see their celebrations, crystal clear in my head, singing and dancing and rubbing it in.

'I know it doesn't matter who the ref is,' I replied. 'I don't care who it is, as long as it's not that –'

Colm's face turned serious. 'That's the end of it,' he interrupted. 'I've warned you before about talking like that – I don't want to hear it. Ever. Okay? You're out there doing your best, and so is the ref. If you're like this now, what are you going to be like on Saturday? You need to be thinking about your game – this game, not the last one. Last season's gone. We lost the league, fair and square. If we were good enough on the day, that last free wouldn't have mattered. Forget about revenge. There's no medals on Saturday anyway.'

'No, but there will be medals at Féile,' I said, determined to have the last word. Every year, there was a big competition to find the best Under-14 team in each county, and then the best Under-14 team in all of Ireland. This year it was our turn – our Féile year. We would only get one shot at it, and it was the only thing that really mattered to any of us. Forget about the league or any of the other competitions. Winning the Dublin Féile for Ballymun, beating all of our rivals from around the city, that was our mission this season.

Féile didn't start until the autumn, though, so Colm was right. In the grand scheme of things, Saturday's match didn't matter. But if we wanted to be the Dublin Féile champions, we'd surely have to beat St Christopher's later on in the summer. Saturday was about showing them that nobody was going to stop us this season.

—

We weren't in any rush home, even if the rain was starting to get a little bit heavier. Kev had brought his own ball with him to training, and the two of us passed it back and forth as we walked, hand passes first, then kick passes as we gradually moved further and further apart. An abandoned shopping trolley lay on its side in the middle of the field, waiting for someone to give it its second life as a makeshift go-kart.

Kev spotted Al and Shane first as they walked towards us, the hoods of their jackets up against the rain. He spotted Shane, really – it was easy enough to pick him out of most crowds. He had always been the tallest of the four of us. Al liked to spike his hair up at the fringe – he thought it made him look a bit taller – but Shane was already easily over six foot and the rest of us weren't anywhere close to that, even on our tippy toes.

Al and Shane both lived in the same block of flats as Kev – the two lads were next-door neighbours on the seventh floor, and Kev was one floor down. It was through Kev that we had all started hanging around a couple of years earlier. Kev's mam, Trish, used to work with Mam in Egan's hardware, so the two of us had been best friends since we were babies. Kev got me to come around one day to play a football match outside their block, and the four of us had been friends ever since.

'Where have the two of yous been?' Al said suspiciously, as if there was some sort of mystery. The knicks and socks should have been a dead giveaway, even if the mucky legs and gear bags weren't.

'Training,' I said. 'It's Thursday.'

'Training. The two of you are always bleedin' training,' Al said, shaking his head as he looked over at Shane. 'I thought it was only on until half seven? We've been walking around for ages looking for you.'

'We were practising our frees afterwards,' Kev explained, 'and then we were just helping Colm bring the gear out to the car.'

'You did more training after training?' Al said, annoyed. 'Lads, the two of you would want to cop on a bit and get a life. Do you just prefer hanging around with your poshie mates or what?'

Shane laughed like he was hearing the joke for the first time, even though we'd had this same stupid conversation a thousand times before. Kev and I were off at training, or playing a match, or up with Colm to watch the Ballymun senior team when they had a match, and Al and Shane didn't like it. I wanted to ask them what the two of them had been doing all evening, what we'd missed that was so important and that had them so upset, even though I knew the answer: nothing. And if they had their way, we would have been there with them, hanging around on the blocks, doing nothing as well.

Al would never admit that, but he knew he'd wind me up by slagging the lads on our team, and I bit.

'You're some muppet,' I snapped back. It wouldn't be our first row over this, and I was sure it wouldn't be our last. 'We play for Ballymun. It's right there in the name, ye thick.'

'Yeah but all of your players aren't from Ballymun, though, are they?' he said with a sneer. 'I'd love to bring them up the flats. I'd say they'd wet themselves.'

The most annoying thing was Al was a very good footballer himself, and so was Shane. They both used to play for Ballymun United, our local soccer team, but in the last year or two, they had lost interest and they could never really explain why. They stopped going to training and, instead, they spent their evenings and weekends hanging around on the blocks, waiting for something to happen.

'Would you not just come up, Al, no?' Kev suggested, not for the first time. 'You'd just need to come training for a few weeks and you'd get your game, no problem.' There was no point even asking Shane. His dad was a die-hard soccer man; he'd never let him play GAA.

'I know I'd get my game,' Al said, angry at the hint that it might not be a foregone conclusion. 'But then what? I'd end up like you? It's your whole bleedin' life. It's all yous ever do.'

We were interrupted before the conversation could go around in circles again. A lad on a bike called out to Al and Shane as he cycled past.

'Yis coming, lads?' He slowed down but didn't stop.

'Five minutes, yeah,' Shane shouted back. 'Get us a few cans?'

'There'll be loads of cans there,' he assured Shane, pulling a wheelie as he zipped off. 'You'll be grand. Just come on before the guards show up.'

'Where are yous going?' Kev asked.

'That's what we were looking for you for,' Al said. 'There's one of the flats up near the top of Eamonn Ceannt that has no one living in it, and Daz Kearns is after getting in and setting it up for a free gaff and a rave.'

The name Daz Kearns was enough to put me off immediately. He was one of that group of older lads I had seen John hanging around with a bit recently. There were loads of stories about him, about how there was a warrant out for him so he'd had to go to England for a few months, or another one about how he'd broken all of the fingers on some fella's hand because he owed him money.

Nobody knew if any of those stories were actually true, but the latest rumour was the one that worried me the most: that when Daz Kearns had come home from England, he had got a job working for Charlie Hanlon.

There was a lot of crime around Dublin, and a lot of criminals, and Charlie Hanlon was the number one. The Godfather. The guards had been trying to put him in jail for 15 years, apparently, but he was always one step ahead of them, careful to never leave any evidence that could connect him to the crime. That was how he was able to hide in plain sight, living right here in Ballymun, where he'd grown up. And although everyone knew his name, I didn't know anyone who had ever actually seen him.

'Are you seriously going hanging around with Daz Kearns?' I asked. If there was even a hint of truth to the rumour, that party was the last place I'd want to be. I prayed that John wasn't going to be there.

'Everyone's going,' Shane said. 'I heard Michelle Flynn's going.' He raised an eyebrow in Kev's direction and made a kissy face. 'You coming?'

Kev gave him the finger.

'Why is there no one in the flat?' I asked.

'Dunno,' Al said. 'I think it was an old woman that died or something, and all of her stuff has been cleaned out so the next people can move in. Daz just busted the door open and he's having a rave there tonight. Come on, stall it up with us for a bit – we won't be there too late.'

He knew there was no way that I'd go, but he still wanted to make me say it.

'Nah, I'm going home. I need to do my boots and have a shower. We're playing Christopher's on Saturday.'

Al couldn't have cared less if I was starting full-back for the Dubs in the All-Ireland final on Saturday. Kev shook his head too. Shane just shrugged his shoulders.

'Suit yourselves,' Al said as the two of them headed off up the road. 'See you tomorrow.'

—

Nobody was home when I got there. The door was locked and all the lights were off inside. When I knocked, there was no answer.

The march. I had forgotten all about it.

I left my bag at the door, went up one more flight of stairs and knocked on the flat directly above ours. I was expecting Mrs O'Dea but it was her husband who answered instead.

'Ah howaya, Philly,' Mr O'Dea said with a smile. 'You're looking for the key, are you?'

Mr and Mrs O'Dea were Ballymun famous. They were both in their seventies now but they were two of the first people to move into the flats when they were built back in the 1960s. On the wall in the hall, there was a newspaper article, framed, with a photo of them and their family on the day they got the keys. Their children had all grown up and moved away but Mr and Mrs O'Dea were still here.

'I'll just unlock the door and I'll drop it back up to you straight away,' I told Mr O'Dea as he handed me out the key. I knew that people who weren't from Ballymun heard about the flats and thought they were this horrible place. And, yeah, of course the blocks could have done with a bit of paint and someone to fix the lifts properly, and there was a bang of wee off the stairwells most of the time, but the flats were our home. I loved that we knew our neighbours so well and that they knew us. I loved that Mr and Mrs O'Dea were like an uncle and aunt to me.

'You're welcome to come in and wait here,' he said. 'It's only me this evening. Rita's gone up to the march as well so I'm sure they'll all be coming home together.'

Mr O'Dea wanted to talk about football, I could tell. He was from Leitrim originally, before he moved up to Dublin for work and met Mrs O'Dea and moved to Ballymun. He was a great storyteller too, particularly when it came to matches he had played in himself, but I was starting to get cold and I had to get changed.

I was already in bed when Mam and Dad came in a little while later, soaked. I had left my door open and Mam came in to me to say goodnight.

'Huge crowd, Philip,' she said, the drops running down off her raincoat and onto the floor. 'It was brilliant. Pity about the rain, a few more people might have come out. No sign of RTÉ either – you'll have to wait until the next time to see me on the news.'

I fell asleep while they were still getting ready for bed, and I don't know what time it was when the voices in the hall woke me up again. Dad's gruff Belfast accent carried through the walls, even when he was doing his best to be quiet.

'Look at the state of you.' He was furious. 'Where the hell have you been?'

'I'm grand, I'm grand,' the voice replied, but John sounded anything but grand. 'Just let me go to bed, will you?'

'Look at me,' Dad ordered.

'I'm grand, I said. I was at a party. I had a few drinks. I'm grand.'

John stumbled in through the bedroom door with a bang. I didn't even open my eyes, pretending to be asleep as he crashed down on the bottom bunk, making the whole bed shake.

I lay awake for a long time, listening to his snores.

5

'Just go out there and enjoy yourselves,' Colm told us as we broke from the huddle and ran out onto the pitch.

Enjoy yourselves. That was always his message. Not 'go out there and win'. Although, for most of us, it was the same thing really.

I went in to the middle of the pitch and shook hands with the referee and the St Christopher's captain. This was my third season as captain, and it was the thing I was most proud of. Colm got to pick 15 players every week, but there could only be one captain. He trusted me. It made me feel special. I had even overheard Mam tell her friends about it once.

'Oh yes, my Philip is doing really well with Ballymun Kickhams,' she boasted. 'And he's the captain.'

We won the coin toss, and I jogged down to the full-back position and touched gloves with Martin in goal. We did it before every game. It was our tradition, for good luck. There was a roar from the sideline – 'COME ON THE SAINTS!'

And the Christopher's players sprinted out to take up their positions alongside us.

Even though they were our biggest rivals, I didn't know most of their names. There was the big lad in midfield who looked like Jesus with the hair down past his shoulders, and they'd had the same goalkeeper for a few years – a bit small for a keeper but good with his kickouts, very accurate.

But I knew who Andrew Devanney was. Dev, everyone called him.

'Yes, Dev, skin him.'

'He can't get near you, Dev. He's chasing shadows.'

'Super score, Dev.'

He was their full-forward, their star, and the player that I always had to mark. His brother was Mick Devanney, the 18-year-old who had just broken through onto the

Dublin senior panel, and everyone said Andrew was even better than his brother had been at that age. He'd had a trial with Arsenal to go over to England and play soccer – they'd offered him a contract, and they'd even brought him and Mick and their dad to meet all of the first-team players – but he decided to stay and play Gaelic instead.

He held out his hand, and as I went to shake it, he grabbed my wrist and pulled me towards him, dipping his shoulder into the centre of my chest with a thump. Before I could even react, the referee blew his whistle and threw the ball in. Game on.

From the other end of the pitch, we watched as Kev scooped up the breaking ball from the throw-in, spun away from his man, and got it in to our half-forwards quickly. Taz got there first and, with a hop, a solo and a flick of his left boot, put the ball over the bar for the first score of the game.

The stinging in my chest only lasted for a second, and by the time it stopped, I had already decided on my next move. It was going to take more than a sneaky hit to put me off my game today. I stood in behind Andrew and waited. When it looked like the ball was about to be played in to us, I gently rested my front stud on the back heel of his boot. He tore off with his hand in the air, shouting and waving for the ball and, as he went, his boot popped loose and flew off.

'Did your mam never teach you how to tie your laces properly, Andrew?' I said as I jogged past him. 'Come over to me at the end and I'll show you how to do it.'

'My name's Dev,' he muttered as he scrambled to pick his boot up and wriggle his foot back into it.

St Christopher's were quick, but we were quicker. We were first to every ball. Every high ball, every 50/50, every scramble, we won them all. Martin took a short kickout to me, exactly as we'd worked on in training, and the pitch opened up in front of me. I took off down the wing. Nobody came to me. I was past the halfway line. All of our lads moved in towards the goal, and their markers all went with them, and I was allowed to keep going and keep going.

There were players out right and out left. I had loads of options, as well as a few on the edge of the square. I let it in, aiming for it to drop on the edge of the square for one of our lads to flick towards goal, but the ball fizzed off the laces of my boot like it was turbo-charged. I watched it, high, long, looping as it dropped over all of the outstretched arms and over the bar for a point.

If a hundred people were there watching us, they made the noise of a full house in Croke Park. The sound was ringing in my ears as I jogged back into position. Mam and June and Lindy and Kellie were in the middle of it all, cheering and clapping. Dad saw me looking over and gave me a thumbs up and then pointed to the side of his head, reminding me not to lose concentration.

Andrew Devanney was standing waiting with his hands on his hips. He hadn't even tried to track back and mark me. He said something to me as I passed him but I was barely listening. I was lost in my own world. I was thinking about John.

—

I had another proper look around the sidelines at half-time but I couldn't see John anywhere. A few people came and went during the second half, but still there was no sign of him. Every time I looked over to where Mam and Dad and the girls were standing, I hoped that he'd have arrived, that he'd be standing there with that big silly smile on his face, loving the fact that we were beating Christopher's.

But no.

John had played GAA himself for a couple of years, mainly for the school team. He was never interested enough to keep it up, but as soon as I started playing, he was my number one fan. He didn't come to every match, but he always knew what was going on, and he was always the first to ask if we had won or not.

I had been talking about this match all week. He'd

promised me that he'd be there. What else could he be doing that was so important?

We were winning by five points at half-time, but the second half was much tighter. Andrew Devanney eventually got one point – a tap-over free, and it wasn't me that fouled him – but that was all, and we won by three in the end.

When we'd shaken hands, Colm pulled all of us into a huddle in the centre circle, clapping each of us on the back as we came in.

'I'll start with the bad news first, lads, and get it out of the way. I've picked a man of the match but unfortunately this week there's no prize.'

Our groans were nearly as loud as any of the cheers during the match. Colm's man of the match prizes were legendary. It was usually a Dublin training top or shorts or socks or a ball or, if he didn't have any football gear that week, he'd give the man of the match a fiver instead. He held up his hand and waited for us all to settle down before he spoke again.

'Martin, brilliant on the kickouts. That was everything we practised in training. You nailed it.'

He made his way around the entire circle, stopping at every player, one by one.

'Super stuff in midfield, Kev. It was like you had the ball on a piece of string.

'Taz, we'll need to change your batteries, they must be burnt out from all of that running.'

Taz's real name was Robert, but everyone called him Taz because he sped around the half-forward line like the Tasmanian Devil cartoon. Colm kept going around the circle and finally he got to me.

'Philly, he didn't have a kick all day.' He didn't even need to say who 'he' was. 'Proper captain's performance, leading by example, great stuff.'

He turned back to speak to everyone. 'There's no way I could just pick one of you out after a performance like that. You're a team, and that was a team win if I ever saw one. So this week, you're all man of the match.'

Quick as a flash, Martin said what we were all thinking. 'Does that mean fivers for everyone so?'

'No, better than that,' Colm said.

'Tenners for everyone?'

'No, there's no money. But that was the bad news,' Colm continued before anyone could interrupt him again, 'and I do have some good news too.' He waited until he was sure we were all listening. 'I got a phone call last night from Gerry Mangan, who is the head of the Dublin academy this year. The trials will be some time around the end of next month, and I've been invited to send our three best players.'

Now he had everyone's undivided attention.

'Lads, you don't need me to tell you what a huge opportunity this is. Every single one of you is good enough for those trials, but I'm only allowed to pick three. So be here for every training session for the next three weeks. Be early. Work hard. Force me to make some impossible decisions. Make sure that you're first on my list when I'm ringing Gerry back with the names.

'Although, after watching you play today,' he added, 'I might just have to tell him that I'll be sending the whole team.'

—

'The Dublin academy, Philip,' Mam said excitedly when the others had gone and it was just the three of us walking towards home. 'That's amazing. What do you think?'

'You were definitely one of the best three out there today,' Dad said. 'I thought Kev was excellent too, and then maybe –'

'Where's John?' I asked, cutting across him.

'I don't know, he didn't tell us,' Dad said. It sounded like an apology, even though it wasn't his apology to make. 'He went out just as we were getting ready to leave. He said he had to go and meet somebody and that he'd better not be late and that he'd follow us down afterwards.'

'Why did he bother promising me he'd come if he was just going to change his mind?' I said, taking a swipe through the top of a dandelion with my foot.

'You'll have to ask him that yourself,' Mam said. 'But I'm sure there's a good reason. He wouldn't let you down like that otherwise.' Even as she said it, she sounded unsure, and all of the excitement had gone from her voice.

I expected to see him long before we got home. I spotted Aaron and Trev over on the steps of the eight-storeys, sitting having a smoke, but there was no sign of John.

I left my boots on the landing outside the flat while I went into the kitchen. Apart from a few bits of muck caught around the studs, they didn't really need to be cleaned, but I'd do them anyway. They were a Christmas present from Mam and Dad, black Adidas Predators, and other than a couple of scuffs on the leather around the instep, they were still as good as the day I first got them. I wanted them to last me forever.

I took the little green bucket out from underneath the sink where I kept it and put it under the hot tap, the sponge bobbing up from the bottom as the water filled it. As I went back outside, I heard a noise coming from my bedroom. The door was half-open, so I pushed it the rest of the way, and there was John, lying on the bottom bunk, still fully dressed, coat and all, and fast asleep. He hadn't even heard us come home.

I should have thrown the bucket of water over him. I was sorely tempted. That would have taught him a lesson. I thumped him on the arm instead, as hard as I could. I wanted him to wake up so I could ask him where he had been, but he barely flinched when I hit him. Only for the fact that his chest was rising and falling, I could have sworn he was dead.

6

John insisted on bringing me into town the following week so he could make it up to me. He was waiting outside the school gates for me when my last class finished on Wednesday afternoon, jingling the coins for the bus fare in his hand, ready to go.

'There's one coming in five minutes,' he said, throwing me a hoodie to put on over my shirt and tie. 'Let's just go now so that we've time to have a proper look in the shops.'

There was a free-for-all at the bus stop as a stream of lads pushed their way on behind us, giddy with freedom.

We were at the top of the queue, though, and while John paid our fares, I ran ahead and saved us seats in the very back row while everyone else piled in, five at a time.

There was so much that I wanted to ask him about the last few weeks. He had been acting strange – even more so since he got sacked from work – but there had to be a simple explanation. Why was he lying to Mam and Dad about getting sacked from work? Who was the dodgy lad who came over to us in the field that night, and what did he want? What was John doing hanging around with Daz Kearns? Why hadn't he shown up for my match? So many things that just didn't add up or make sense, but it was never the right time to ask him. There was always someone else there, one of his friends or one of my friends, and I knew he'd never tell me the story straight unless it was just the two of us alone.

I couldn't ask now either. The bus had gone from practically empty to full in the blink of an eye, and there were far too many people around who would hear every word of our conversation. Besides, we hadn't been into town together in a while, just the two of us, and I could tell John was excited to be bringing me out. Instead, I told him Colm's news about the Dublin academy trials.

'I'll still be training with Ballymun but I'll have to go academy training once a week as well,' I said, bursting into detail. If this was what we were talking about,

I didn't mind if the whole bus was listening. 'And then sometimes, I heard, you go for a weekend camp where it's Saturday and Sunday and you stay overnight.' There was no stopping me once I'd started. Poor John couldn't get a word in edgeways. 'And some of the Dublin players come down and do coaching sessions and skills sessions' – I knew that bit because Colm had told me – 'and then you have matches against the other counties, and you actually play for Dublin, and they give you your own kit and tracksuit and everything, but they only have thirty places or something in the academy every year, so it's a really big deal.'

John laughed at that last bit while I caught my breath again. 'I know it's a really big deal,' he said. 'Who do you think Colm will pick to send with you to the trials?'

'What? I might not even get picked as one of the three,' I said. 'There's no guarantee. We've loads of good players this season. You should have seen us on Saturday –'

I regretted saying it as soon as the words were out of my mouth. John had apologised, and even though he hadn't really explained why he'd missed the match or what had him so tired, I knew he still felt bad.

'Of course you'll be one of the three,' he assured me. 'I know loads of them are good, but none of them are as good as you.'

Hearing that from John made me feel ten feet tall.

'You don't know that, though,' I argued. 'You're only saying that because you're my brother.'

'Yeah, maybe you're right,' he conceded, looking out the window at the stopped traffic alongside us. 'But you never know, maybe I'm right too.'

—

Going into town together had always been our thing, from the time I was six or seven. The three girls, June, Lindy and Kellie, always went together, but John and I were never too interested in joining them. We liked to do our own thing, which was John's thing really. I followed him around his favourite shops, looking at the brightest tracksuits, the whitest runners, the best CDs, and I learned about the world and what was cool and what wasn't.

Some days, Aaron would come with us too. The two of them had been put sitting beside each other on the first day of school and had been best friends ever since. John always wanted to look in the dance music section in the music shop, or in the American rap section to see if there were any new Tupac CDs. Aaron would leave us at it – wandering off to the Bob Marley section, probably – but if John was into dance music and rap, then so was I.

I was starving by the time we got off the bus, and as soon as I hinted at getting something to eat, John disappeared and then reappeared just as quickly, handing me a brown paper bag that felt like it was ready to burst. Inside was a cheeseburger, which smelled as delicious as it looked, a carton of chips that was already overflowing in the bag like a fast-food treasure chest, a chocolate milkshake and a little plastic tub of ice-cream. I was down to the last bite of my burger when I realised that John hadn't bought any food for himself.

'Don't worry about me,' he told me, picking a few chips out of the bottom of my bag. 'You eat away there, I'm grand. I had lunch before I picked you up.'

Maybe it was just the clothes he was wearing, but sitting beside me, John looked even skinnier than usual. He had always been the tall one of the family, and never had much in the way of muscle, but now his tracksuit was falling off him with no shape at all underneath it, like it had been left sitting loose over a wire hanger. It wasn't normal. I was worried that he might be sick and hadn't told me, but I didn't want to bring it up now, not when he had gone to all this trouble to bring me out for the afternoon. I made a note in my head to ask Mam and Dad about it later.

'Come on, I want to have a look in here,' he said when I had finished my ice-cream, pointing towards the sports shop. I went straight over to the sale bin for the football jerseys, rummaging through the pile to see if there was anything in my size. Everton and Celtic were John's two teams, so that was who I supported too.

'This one's mad, John – look,' I said, digging right down to the bottom and pulling out a fluorescent orange jersey. I didn't recognise the team crest, I couldn't even make out what country it was from, so I started to check the labels for a clue. 'Where do you think this is from?'

He took it out of my hand and had a quick look before putting it back into the pile. 'Don't mind that for a minute. Try this one on instead,' he said, and he handed me a Dublin jersey. 'Try it on,' he said again, looking over his shoulder towards the front door. 'Otherwise they're going to think we're only in here messing and they'll kick us out.'

'I got given out to the last time in here for trying jerseys on because they said I wasn't buying anything,' I said.

He pushed me over towards a mirror. 'Just. Try. It. On.'

I took my hoodie off and pulled the jersey on. I had a Dublin T-shirt and a training top that Colm had given me, but I didn't have an actual jersey. It smelled brand new, like it had just come out of its plastic packaging. I took a look in the mirror. It looked a bit funny with the collar of the jersey and then the collar of my school shirt underneath it, but other than that, it was perfect.

'It suits you,' John said, standing back so he could get a proper look. 'It's the right size and everything. Take it off there so we can bring it up to the till and pay for it.'

I didn't want to take it off. I wanted to wear it out of the shop right there and then. But I couldn't let John buy it for me.

'Don't worry,' I said. 'We don't need to get it now.' He seemed disappointed. 'You can get it for me some other time,' I suggested as a compromise, 'when you're back working again.'

But he persisted. 'Stop, would you? I have the money – I'm buying it for you. You can't just walk out with it like that,' he said. 'Unless ...' A grin of mischief crept over his face as he lowered his voice. 'Well, you probably could if you wanted to, but you'd need to be ready to run.' He looked towards the door out of the corner of his eyes. 'They might catch me but you're quick enough to get away.'

The panicked look on my face made him laugh.

'Relax, relax, I'm only messing,' he said, holding out his hand for the jersey. 'I want to get it for you. Anyway, it's the only time I'll ever have to buy you a Dublin jersey.'

'What do you mean?' I asked.

'By the time you grow out of this one, you'll be on one of those Dublin squads and you'll be like Colm

Doyle, getting more free jerseys and gear than you're able to use. You'll be giving the stuff away.'

I liked the sound of that, but still, I couldn't let him buy it. I took the jersey off and hung it back up on the rail that he'd taken it from.

'It's okay, don't worry about it. I'll just have to get on a squad soon,' I said, dragging him out of the shop before he could change my mind. 'Come on, let's go, that security guard is starting to look at us funny.'

We went in and out of shops for the rest of the afternoon, looking at football boots and tracksuits and runners, some of which we couldn't have afforded even in our wildest dreams. But it was nice to look. John didn't mention the jersey again.

'I've an idea,' he said when the shops started to close. It was still early, still bright outside, and neither of us was ready to go home yet. As we turned to walk up O'Connell Street, I knew exactly where he was heading. The Savoy, the big old cinema, was one of our favourite places to go on our trips into town together. We hadn't been there for a long time but we did the same as always: I waited outside while John went in and bought the tickets, and then I snuck in before anyone noticed that I wasn't 15 or 18 or whatever age I was supposed to be to see the film.

John went up to the counter and asked for two for whatever was starting next. I liked spy stories with a bit of action in them, and this one was good, even though I didn't recognise any of the actors in it. And when it was over, we broke away from the queue of people walking out to the exit and snuck into the screen next door. We spent most of the film asking each other questions – it was already halfway through by the time we sat down in the back row, and neither of us could work out the story, but we were more interested in just having a laugh ourselves anyway. We left before it was over and walked across the road to wait for the bus home.

It was late by the time we got back to Ballymun, but the streets and the field were still humming with groups dotted around in threes and fours. A few blocks down from ours, there was a faint orange glow and a familiar fuss. The bin chute, the long metal tube that ran from the top floor to the bottom in each block of flats, had been set on fire again. A woman in her dressing-gown tipped a basin of water in on top of the flames before they could spread any further, and the smell of burning rubbish hung in the air.

At home, everyone was in bed. Mam and Dad were still awake, the light creeping out from under their bed-room door. I climbed up into bed and fell asleep before my head hit the pillow, tired but happy.

7

I started the argument the night John was put out of the flat.

When I opened the tin and saw that my money was missing, I could have just said nothing. But I didn't.

I wasn't saving up for anything in particular. I just liked saving. It was mostly money that I'd got from Dad, pocket money, two euro a week, for doing my chores at home. Sometimes, Dad wouldn't have any coins, he'd only have a fiver, so he'd pay me double and let me keep the extra euro.

'That's your bonus,' he'd say, and I'd take it and put it straight into my piggy bank. It wasn't a real piggy bank, one of those ones that was actually shaped like a pig, round and pink with a little hole in its back for the money. It was a tin box, the same size as a book but a lot thicker, and it had the Everton crest on it. I'd been filling it for about a year and a half; John had bought me the new Everton jersey for Christmas that year out of his bonus from the Meat Packers, and he had wrapped the piggy bank inside the jersey as an extra little surprise.

Once you'd put the money in, you couldn't just open it up to take some out again whenever you liked. You had to cut the tin open to get at it. That was a bit of a waste because you could only use the tin once, but the people who made them probably liked it because then you had to buy a new one so you could start all over again. So I never opened it, and once the money went in, it stayed there.

I loved feeling the tin getting heavier and heavier. Fivers didn't weigh anything, that was the best part, and I knew there was a load of them in there. I'd move the tin from hand to hand just so I could feel the coins sliding from one side to the other. And then I'd put it back in its hiding place, in the orange and brown Nike shoebox buried underneath some old T-shirts at the bottom of the wardrobe.

That night, I took it out of the wardrobe and put it down in the middle of the floor. The rattle of the coins made me happy. I had thought about opening it every day for the last three weeks. After we had looked at the jerseys and the tracksuits and the runners in town that day, John and I had gone in to the big mobile phone shop on Henry Street. None of my friends had a phone yet, but I thought that maybe I could be the first. Al kept saying that his parents had promised to get him one for his birthday, but that wasn't until October, which was after mine. A few of the lads in school had got this really cool one, a Nokia 3210, and they were always showing off in the yard about the games you could play on it and sending each other messages under the desk when the teacher wasn't looking.

But the man in the shop had shown me an even newer version that had just come out, the Nokia 3310. Once I saw it, I knew I wanted it. Everyone would be mad jealous then. I couldn't ask Mam and Dad to get it – I knew Mam had her little purple tin, but that money was for when I needed new football boots – so I decided to count out my money to see if I could buy it for myself.

I took a tin opener from the drawer in the kitchen and brought it back into my room. I didn't want to spend the money. I just wanted to see how much was there and how much more I needed to save. The coins spilled out into a pile on the bedroom floor, like in one of those slot machines in the arcade. One or two tried to escape, rolling over towards the radiator, but I stuck my foot out to stop them. I ran my hand through the top of the little hill, spreading them out and getting ready to count, when I noticed something missing.

It was all coins. There were no notes.

I picked the tin back up and checked it again, hoping they'd all somehow fallen to the bottom and got stuck. There was nothing there. Where had they gone? There was no other way to open the tin, and there were no signs of any marks on it. It was a mystery but I knew the first place I had to look.

John was the only person who knew where I kept the tin. He had seen me put it back into its box in the wardrobe one night, and he'd promised me he wouldn't say a word to anyone. Kellie had gone out with a few of her friends, and when I burst into the sitting room, John was sitting watching TV by himself.

'Did you take my money?' I snapped, turning the tin on its side so he could see it was empty.

'No,' he said, sounding surprised. 'What money?'

I stood between him and the TV. 'All the notes are gone out of my money box. I know you took it. Nobody else even knows where I hide it.'

There was no point in me jumping on top of him and starting a fight. I was strong for my age, but John was a man.

'Give it back to me, John,' I begged, more out of desperation than anger. 'Where is it?'

He blanked me again. 'I don't know what you're talking about. I didn't touch your money.'

If we had just settled it ourselves, everything would have been grand, but I knew John was lying to me. I only had one other option. 'I'm telling Mam,' I said.

'No, don't, Philly. Wait.' There was panic in his voice as he got up out of his chair. He knew he was going to be in trouble. 'I have it. I'll get it for you.'

But it was already too late. When I ran back out of the room, shouting, he didn't try to follow me or stop me.

'Mam,' I cried. She came out of her bedroom, her arms full of clothes ready to go into the wash.

'Stop screaming, would you?' she said. 'What's wrong with you?'

'John's after robbing all of my money out of my tin and it's gone and he won't give it back to me.'

'What?'

I repeated myself, except this time more slowly. 'My money. It's gone. I opened up my tin to count it because I wanted to see how much more I need to save to buy a phone, but when I opened it all of the notes were gone and it's only the coins left.' I brought her over to my bedroom door and pointed at the coins, still in a mound in the middle of the floor. 'Look!'

The look on Mam's face changed, as if I'd just told her some really bad news and it had taken her a moment to understand it. She put the clothes down in the middle of the hall and took me by the arm to go back into the sitting room. John was standing where I had left him.

'Where's Philip's money, John?' she demanded. She didn't even ask if he was the one who had taken it. She still had a tight hold on my arm, so I could feel her shaking.

John started to speak but the front door opened before he could get any words out, and Dad came in. He had been outside talking to Mags Flynn, who lived next door, when he heard us arguing. He looked at me and John and then, lastly, to Mam. 'What's the shouting for?' he asked her.

'John's after stealing Philip's money from his money box,' she explained. The room suddenly felt quite small with the four us there, all standing so close to one another. Mam wasn't finished with John yet. 'Don't make me ask you twice. Where is it?'

'I just took a loan of it,' he blurted out. 'I'm sorry. I was going to put it back in the tin before he even knew it was missing. I'll put it back, I promise.'

Once I knew I was going to get it back, that was all I cared about. I didn't like how worked up everyone was getting. I just wanted to the argument to be over and everyone to go back to what we'd been doing five minutes earlier.

Mam kept going. 'Put it back now then,' she told John, moving aside so he could get past her and go and get it. 'Go on. Where is it?'

'I don't have it right now,' he said helplessly. 'I spent it. I'll get it back for you, Philly, don't worry.'

Dad hadn't budged from where he was standing in front of the door, and there was nowhere for John to go. When Dad finally spoke, his voice was loudest of all. 'What else did you take, John?'

The colour drained out of John's face. He started fidgeting nervously, rolling and unrolling the sleeves of his track top. 'What? Nothing. Nothing.'

It wasn't convincing, and Dad repeated himself, slowly and deliberately. 'What else did you take, John?'

John looked like he was about to burst into tears as he looked in Mam's direction.

'Jesus, John,' she said with a fright. She had been holding on to my arm this whole time but now she let go, pushed past Dad and ran to her room. She was back three seconds later, an open empty wooden box in her hand. 'Where is it, John? Where's all my jewellery gone?'

She didn't wait for an answer. She grabbed her purse from the arm of the couch and she was gone, not wanting to waste a second.

'Wait, Ma. I'll fix it,' John called out.

I went after her. I couldn't stay in that room any longer. I didn't want to be near John. I couldn't even look at him. A million possibilities ran through my head and none of them seemed like good situations. Whatever this was about, whatever trouble he was after getting himself into, him and Dad could sort it out between themselves. They didn't need me there.

'Mam, what's going on? Where are you going?' I asked as I caught up with her going down the stairs.

She wiped the corners of her eyes with the back of her hand. 'I'm grand, Philip. You go on back home.'

'I'm coming with you,' I insisted, even though I didn't know where we were going. Mam did, though. She went straight around the corner and up the stairwell into one of the eight-storey blocks, the one next to where Kev and Al and Shane lived. On the bottom floor, the doors of the lift were covered in stickers and graffiti. It had been years since they had been properly cleaned. Even the sign stuck to the front – Temporarily Out of Order – had torn and mostly fallen off.

Mam went up four, maybe five, flights of stairs, turned left, stopped at the first flat that we came to and hammered on the front door, still clutching her purse in front of her.

'Whose flat is this?' I asked nervously as she knocked for a second time.

'Ssssh. Just stand there beside me,' she said, and then quickly added, 'If anything happens, you're to run and get your dad.'

We didn't have time to get into the details of what was she concerned might happen. Once she realised nobody was coming to answer the door to her, she turned and left, but we weren't going home.

We didn't speak in the two minutes it took us to get to the next block of flats. I'd no idea what Mam was thinking, and so many questions were rattling around in my head that I wouldn't even know where to start. Again, when we got there, Mam knew exactly which door she was looking for. This time, a man opened the door – not all the way, but just enough that he could see us through the crack.

It was a month since I'd seen him but I recognised him immediately, even without the baseball cap pulled down over his eyes and the big dark duffel coat. He was the guy who had been looking for John that night when we were sitting out in the field.

There was a funny smell from his flat, and I wrinkled my nose. Mam got straight to the point without any introduction. 'Do you have my jewellery?' she said, trying to push the door open slightly to see the man fully. It was locked with a chain on the inside, which stopped it sharply.

'Did my son sell you my jewellery?' she asked again.

'I don't know what you're talking about,' the man said angrily. He eyed me up, standing there by Mam's side, but if he recognised me, he didn't show it.

'You know exactly what I'm talking about,' Mam said, not ready to take no for an answer. 'I'm not here looking for a row. I just want my jewellery back.'

He moved to close the door. 'I don't know what you're doing here,' he said. 'I don't have any jewellery.'

Mam unzipped her purse and started to pull notes out of it. 'I'll buy it back from you,' she said, holding them tightly in her closed fist. 'I'll give you whatever money he owes you. I just want my things back.'

The man's tone changed a bit at the sight of the money in Mam's hand, but he shook his head. 'Look, I don't have it,' he said. 'If I did, I'd sell it to you. I'd prefer the money anyway. Jewellery's no use to me, really, it's only more hassle. But I don't have it. He doesn't even owe me any money at the minute. It must be someone else that has your stuff.'

Mam sank as he shut the door in our faces, like someone was after pointing a remote control at her and pressing the off button. She stood on the landing without moving, all of her attention fixed on the closed door, until I took her hand and gave it a little squeeze to make sure she was okay. She looked at me, the tears gathering in her eyes, and then put the notes back into her purse and slowly zipped it up.

'Come on, Philip,' she said as she led me back down the stairs. We walked to the end of the road and she looked up towards the Towers, but then she thought better of it and turned around towards home.

'Was it all in the box, Mam?' I asked quietly, afraid to even hear the answer. 'All of your jewellery, I mean?'

She swallowed hard and nodded.

'Even your bracelet?'

She didn't nod this time, but I knew the answer was yes.

Mam didn't have a lot of jewellery, except for one or two nice necklaces and a few sets of earrings that she loved to take out whenever there was a special occasion. But the one piece of jewellery that meant the most to her was the gold bracelet that Nanny, her mam, had given her when she was a little girl.

Whatever was going on with John, whatever trouble he was in, I couldn't forgive him for doing this to her.

When we got home again, Dad was sitting in his chair, warming his hands on a cup of tea that looked like it had barely been touched. He didn't even look up as we came in.

Mam went to sit down beside him, and I went into my room and slammed the door behind me. The whole flat shook with the noise, but the whole block could have come crashing down around us for all I cared. Someone shouted, the kind of roar that you can tell a person has no control over, that they just need to let out, and then I realised that it was me. It didn't make me feel any better.

I stepped around the pile of coins, still sitting in the middle of the floor where I'd left them, and opened my football bag to check for my boots. They had cost a lot of money when Mam and Dad bought them for me – they were still worth a bit of money, even second-hand – and the thought had crossed my mind for a second as we were walking. They were still there, but the rest of the room felt a bit more empty than usual. And I could tell by the bits that were missing that John was gone.

I was about to go inside to Mam and Dad when I spotted a paper bag sitting on my bed, on top of my pillow. I lifted it down and looked inside, then took out the plastic packet so I could take a proper look.

It was a brand-new Dublin jersey, in my size. The very one that we had been looking at in the shop, the one that I told him not to buy. I didn't want it now, not after everything that had happened. It made me angry just holding it. I quickly put it back in the bag and pushed it into the back of the wardrobe, where I wouldn't have to look at it.

It was only then that I noticed the note left with it, still sitting on my pillow. I unfolded it. It had

been scribbled in a hurry but it was definitely John's
handwriting:

*I'm sorry, Philly. I'll get you the money back, I
promise. Stay out of trouble and be good for
Mam and Dad. I'll see you soon. Don't worry
about me.*

Love you bro,
J

8

was glad when Kellie knocked to see if I was okay. The silence was starting to hurt my head.

'Mam and Dad told me what happened,' she said, quietly because everything was quiet. 'Come inside and sit down with us for a while.' She left the door open behind her, expecting me to follow.

I don't know how I long I had been sitting there on the edge of the bottom bunk. It might have been half an hour, it might have been more. When we came home and John was gone, there was no more shouting, no more crying. It was like a bonfire with a can of petrol poured over it: once the match was dropped, everything exploded and ran wild, unstoppable. But now all that was left were the last grey ashy bits and a few puffs of smoke, and the quiet was making me more anxious and uneasy, not less.

My mind was racing. John had definitely been acting strange these last few weeks. While I was on my own, I had forced myself to think about the best possible explanations for what had just happened – for what was happening. But for him to have stolen Mam's jewellery, for him to do something that would hurt the one person he loved more than anyone in the world so badly, there were only bad options.

And now, as all the pieces of the jigsaw slowly started to fit together in the back of my mind, I knew that even if I'd prefer not to know the truth, I couldn't run away from it either. I didn't have a choice. I crumpled up the note that John had left me – I was too angry with him to even think about that – and I went into the sitting room.

'Are you okay?' I asked Mam. I was worried about her most of all. Her eyes were red and raw, and she dabbed at them with the tissue in her hand, shaking her head.

'No,' she said, although she nearly swallowed it instead of saying it. It killed me to see her so upset. Dad sat opposite her, holding her hand across the table, staring without looking at anything in particular.

'We thought we could help him to get better,' she said when she eventually spoke again. 'We thought he'd be okay. He told us he was doing all of the things he was supposed to be doing, that he was clean again ...'

Clean.

Everything changed in one single word as Mam's voice trailed off. I had been hoping against hope for another explanation – maybe it was one of John's friends who was in trouble, and his only real mistake was doing something stupid when he tried to help him out – but deep down, I was afraid that it was this.

That it was drugs.

'What is it, Mam?' I said, but it barely came out as a whisper.

She looked so tired as she turned to me. 'It's heroin, Philip.'

It hit me like a punch. Ballymun had lots of problems and lots of drugs, and none of them were good, but heroin was the worst. Heroin meant havoc.

It meant calling over for Kev or Al or Shane, but having to walk past someone injecting themselves right there in the stairwell, in broad daylight, in the middle of the day, not caring that they were surrounded by kids coming and going and playing.

It meant dirty needles left lying in the grass that Mam had begged us never to go near since we were old enough to walk.

It meant pushers and protests. It meant zombies on the blocks and in the field, barely able to stand or to form a full sentence. It meant mugging people for a few euro, or less, because that was the only way.

It meant overdoses. It meant ambulances. It meant funerals after funerals, men and women, boys and girls, John's age, younger, gone too soon.

I had seen how it united the people of Ballymun, desperately doing everything we could to keep this wolf from the door. And now here it was, right here in our sitting room.

So when Mam spoke, it felt like a death sentence.

'Is he going to be all right?' Kellie had been sitting listening, and then asked the only question that mattered.

Mam paused and took a deep breath before answering. 'We thought we were doing okay,' she said. 'He told me he was off it. I wanted to bring him around to the Brickhouse to see someone, to see if we could get him a bit of help, but he didn't want to go. He said he didn't need it, that he wasn't bad enough to be going around there. I think he thought he could manage it himself. He promised me he wouldn't touch it for a few weeks and that would be enough, that he'd never go near it again then.'

My heart sank even further at the mention of the Brickhouse. That was what everyone called the drug treatment centre in Ballymun. It was a big old building on the other side of the main road. I had never been inside it, and I never wanted to be. It was a horrible, hopeless place.

'That place is awful,' I said out loud without even realising. The people who went there for help all seemed so empty, like they had been taken apart and every bit of life in them had been scooped out. John couldn't possibly be that bad. We couldn't possibly be talking about him needing to go there.

But we were.

'How long has he been like this?' I asked.

'A year,' Dad said. 'Maybe a bit longer than that. We thought it was just drink at first. He'd lie to us when he came in and say that he'd just been having cans with the lads, but soon we knew that wasn't it. We could tell by the way he was acting. I thought he might have been smoking or something.'

'Did you know anything about this?' I asked Kellie. She was tracing a pattern on the table with her finger while she listened.

'No,' she said. 'I wish I did.'

'How was he able to keep hiding it?' As I said it, a second thought occurred to me. 'He wasn't doing it here, was he?' The flat was big enough for the five of us but too small for secrets. I had always shared a bedroom with him.

'No, I don't think he'd ever do that,' Mam said, but I wasn't too sure. We'd never spoken about the day he missed my match, when I'd come home and found him lying there asleep in all of his clothes – asleep or passed out? Now wasn't the time for me to bring it up.

'He's very good at hiding it,' Mam continued. 'I always thought, looking at those poor divils out on the street and all of their families, that it would be obvious, that he'd let something slip by accident or there'd be some sort of clue, that we'd just know by the way he was. But there was never anything really. I don't know.'

All of those nights I'd spent out in the field with John and his friends, I knew that there were two Johns really: the John when I was there hanging around with them, not exactly trying to be a good influence, but definitely trying not to give me too many bad habits; and then the other John, who could do what he wanted when I was gone home to bed. He didn't mind if I saw him having a can or two of beer or cider, but he'd never get drunk when I was with him, even though I'd heard him stumble in to bed on plenty of occasions. If I was there when his friends were smoking hash, he made sure that I noticed him passing on the joint without taking a drag himself, but once you know the smell, it's hard to miss it, and there were nights when it followed him in the door, stuck to his clothes like glue. Maybe that's just what big brothers do; they hide things from their little brothers.

But even though heroin was all around us, right there on our doorstep, I'd never once heard him or any of his friends suggest it, not even as a joke when they were fed up and making dares to see how far they could push each other before someone backed down.

'I warned him so many times,' Dad said. 'It's lethal. He didn't even realise himself. He told me that he didn't think it would do any harm because it was only a little bit.'

'He came in one night and he was bad,' Mam explained. 'Your dad checked his pockets. He didn't have any drugs – I think he knew better than to bring them into this flat – but he had little strips of tinfoil that he was using to smoke the heroin and your dad found them. There was no point in him lying to us then. We're not stupid.'

She let the tears roll down her face now. The tissue had practically disintegrated in her hand, and she wasn't bothered with it anymore.

'We can't help him if we don't know what's going on,' she said, her voice breaking. 'I don't care what mistakes he's made. I just want him to tell us so we can help him get better. How many flats have we gone into to say we're sorry to heartbroken mas and das? All those poor families. How many funerals have you all been to?'

I thought she was going to start listing them out but she didn't. She didn't need to. We knew exactly who she was talking about.

'Promise me,' she begged us, looking at me and Kellie like we were the only two people left in the world. 'Promise me now, both of you, that you'll never touch it. You'll never think about it. You'll never even look at it. Because I can't. I just can't –'

The worry came pouring out of her in floods of tears. Kellie moved to sit beside her and put her arm around her, hugging Mam into her side while she cried on her shoulder. Every sob was like a knife. Wherever John was, I hoped he knew what he had done.

'Where is he now?' I asked Dad. Part of me wanted to go and find him and bring him back so he could see for himself the world that he had turned upside down.

'I don't know where he went,' Dad said. 'I just told him to pack his bags and be gone before you and your mam came home. We had this conversation with him before. We told him that he wasn't welcome here if he was still using drugs. If he was going to live here, he had to be clean. They were the rules.'

'Who is he going to stay with, though?' Kellie said.

'Let him figure it out,' Dad snapped. He leaned forward in the chair, his elbows resting on his knees, his right hand pinching the bridge of his nose so that we couldn't see his face. It was a good question. If I ever needed somewhere to stay, Kev's would be the first place that I'd try; maybe Aaron would let John stay.

'We didn't put him out because we don't love him,' Mam said. 'We love him to bits. That's why we're doing it. But he has to understand, it's either us or the heroin. He can't have both. He has to choose. I can't do another night lying awake in bed waiting for him to come in, wondering if he'll come or if he's lying in a stairwell somewhere. I can't be afraid to answer the door every time there's a knock in case it's a guard standing there with bad news. I can't do it. I'm not able.'

'It's the only way,' Dad agreed. 'If he's here and he's using, and now he's stealing too, and we let it keep happening, we're killing him. He'll never get better. It'll just get worse and worse.'

'I just don't know how he's managed to keep going with work this whole time,' Mam said.

I jumped in. 'He's not working. He got sacked about a month ago.'

I told them about walking home with John that day after the fight up at the Monos and how he'd told me

83

not to say anything. I felt stupid now for keeping his secrets for him. More than stupid, I felt guilty, like this all could have been avoided if Mam and Dad knew that John was out of work and struggling for money.

And when I was finished, I told them about the night when he had been threatened out in the field.

'It was the same man whose flat we called to tonight,' I said to Mam. 'Is that who's dealing to him?'

Mam frowned at the mention of him, or maybe it was at the thought of her missing jewellery. 'No, he just collects the money. He was always hassling Claire Mac's Wayne when he was alive – that's how I know where he lives. He's a nasty one, though, threatened them with all sorts if they didn't pay up.'

'He's only a little runt of a gofer,' Dad muttered. 'One of Charlie Hanlon's crew, I'm sure. They're all little bloodsuckers, those lads. I know plenty that would love to meet them in a dark alley some night, see how brave they are then.'

Just hearing the name Charlie Hanlon was enough to make me shiver.

'Anyway,' Mam said, 'you're to stay well away if you see him around again, do you hear me?'

I promised her that I would. I didn't want to ever see the man again. I didn't want any of this. All I wanted was for life to go back to normal.

The clock beside the fridge ticked and ticked, and as the four of us sat there and everything sank in, I realised that life hadn't been normal for a long time, a lot longer than I had known.

9

Kev and I stood at the gates and looked up nervously at the big cold building staring back down at us. We had been standing there for at least five minutes and nobody had gone into the building or come out of it. Every window had a shutter pulled down tight on the inside and, at the top of the stone steps, the front door was shut. For all we knew, the place was empty, closed for the day. The three or four cars parked up on the tarmac driveway in the front were the only clue that suggested otherwise.

The steel sign beside the front door had turned dull long ago. If you didn't know anything about the Brickhouse, about the people who needed it, you wouldn't have guessed much by looking at it from the outside.

'Do you wanna go in?' Kev asked me as he eyed up the windows for any signs of movement. We had walked by this place hundreds of times, but normally from a safe distance on the opposite side of the road, and this was the closest we'd ever been to the inside.

I looked around. The usual Wednesday-afternoon mix of cars and people were going about their business, not paying us the slightest bit of attention. I was more worried about bumping into someone from school, someone who knew us and might ask us what we were up to. Al and Shane had walked out with us when we were finished for the day. I'd told them we were going to collect something for Colm, and they'd rolled their eyes and gone off home.

It was two weeks since Mam and Dad had put John out of the flat, and Kev was the only person I had told about what had happened. It had been his idea for us to come up here. The two of us had been friends forever; he didn't have any brothers or sisters, and he was the closest thing I had to a brother my own age. I told him the whole story of that night – the money, the jewellery and the conversation in the sitting room afterwards

– because I could trust him not to tell anyone. I didn't want anyone feeling sorry for me or looking at me and thinking I was going to end up doing heroin too. I didn't think what was happening in our family was anyone else's business. Besides, it was Ballymun; everyone would know soon enough anyway. Secrets never stayed secret for long.

'Come on, are we going in?' Kev asked me again.

'For what?'

'This isn't bleedin' Macari's – we're not going in for a quarter-pounder and chips,' he said, shaking his head at the stupid question. 'What do you think we're going in for? To ask them.'

'Ask them what?'

'I dunno,' he said with a bit of frustration. 'Ask them all these questions that you're asking me. Ask them the stuff that you're worried about. They'll know the answers.'

I had been asking Kev a lot of questions. It was the only way I could stop worrying. I didn't expect him to know the answers any more than I knew them myself, but at least by asking them, it was getting them out of my head and into the world and freeing up a little more space in my brain, which was starting to feel more and more like a squeezed sponge these last few days.

But the Brickhouse was for people with a drug addiction, not for their little brothers. I couldn't just walk in and expect someone to hand me a leaflet that said 'My brother's using heroin. What do I do now?' on the front of it.

'No,' I said, hesitating. 'Come on, let's go.' But I didn't move to leave, and neither did Kev. 'Do you think they have someone who I could talk to?' I asked. 'They'll probably just think we're on the wind-up.'

Kev stared at me as if I'd lost my mind. 'How many people do you think go into a drug treatment centre' – he paused, pointing at the crest on his jumper – 'in their school uniforms and ask for information about heroin as a wind-up?'

Well, when you put it like that, I thought.

He started to move towards the door, waiting for me to join him. 'There might not be anyone there today,' he said. 'Or maybe they don't have anyone who does stuff like that. But at least you'll have asked. Come on anyway, let's go in or let's go home. This place freaks me out.'

He'd said it before he could catch himself. It was true; it freaked me out too. It just wasn't particularly helpful to hear it.

'Sorry,' he said with an apologetic smile.

He was right, though. I had nothing to lose by asking, so I took a deep breath and walked across the driveway and up the steps to the front door before I changed my mind again. I pushed it, hoping that it might swing open and we could let ourselves in without making a scene. A few flakes of chipped red paint came away in my hand, but the door was heavy and it didn't budge.

I looked for a doorbell or a buzzer but I couldn't see one. There was an old brass knocker, though, and just as I reached for it, I heard voices on the other side of the door and the sound of a key in a lock.

'Sketch,' I hissed at Kev, panicking, as I turned and ran without a second thought. I don't know why we hid – go with what you know, I suppose – as if we were about to do something wrong by knocking on the door and asking for help. We ducked in between two of the parked cars just as the door swung open and a woman came out onto the top step.

When the door closed behind her, she was by herself. She was a young woman, no more than five or six years older than John, but she moved slowly and uncertainly, with a shuffle rather than a step, which made her look much older than she was. She should have been tall but she wasn't standing fully straight, hunched over as if the faded shopping bag in her left hand carried the weight of the world. Her hair was tied back into a ponytail but it made her face – her eyes, her nose, her lips – sink back into itself like little dots and lines. She looked frail, skinny, as she sat down on the steps, no more than a couple of metres away from where we were, and started to cry.

I watched as she put her head in her hands, talking to herself quietly in between sobs. Even though this was a place where people came to get help, everything about the Brickhouse was grim and miserable and made me anxious. That uneasy feeling twisted inside me, getting worse as I watched this poor woman crying alone on the steps. I didn't want to be there any more. We needed to get out.

'Should we check if she's okay?' Kev mouthed, but I shook my head. We couldn't suddenly pop out from our hiding place to ask if she was all right – we would frighten the life out of her – but I also knew there was no way for us to leave without being noticed either. Our only option was to stay where we were and wait for her to go. It was obvious that she needed help, but nobody was coming to help her, and neither would we; that made me feel even worse.

When she got up and left after a few minutes, I was ready to go home too. Maybe the people in the Brickhouse would be able to help me, but I'd come back another day. As I stood up and went to come out from between the cars, Kev grabbed me by the arm and pulled me back down beside him, pointing over to the gates.

The woman was still standing there as a man cycled

up beside her. His tracksuit was pristine, every bit as flashy as his bike. It was hard to know which was more expensive. The woman's face froze when she saw him. She knew him but she wasn't happy to see him.

'No, no, no,' she said. 'Just go away, would you? I told you already to leave me alone.'

'What sort of a welcome is that?' the man said, but he was the only one who found it funny. 'I have your stuff for you. What do you want and I'll go and get it for you now?'

They were only standing a couple of feet apart, but they were speaking at the tops of their voices, loud enough for anyone to hear.

'Leave me alone,' the woman said, agitated, needing to get away from this conversation as quickly as possible. She went to walk past him but the man rolled his bike out in front of her, blocking her way.

'What's that in your hand?' he said, snatching a piece of paper away from her before she could respond.

'No, I need that, give it back,' she pleaded, unable to hide the desperation in her voice. 'I've to go up to the chemist to get that.'

The man wasn't interested, moving his arm out of her reach as he unfolded the note. 'The chemist?' he said, mocking her. 'Let me have a look so and see what you're getting.' He read it aloud. 'Methadone? Did they tell you that would help get you off the heroin? They're full of it. You're wasting your time with that stuff. It's not going to do anything for you.' His tone changed and he suddenly sounded a lot less aggressive and a lot more friendly. 'Don't worry, I'll sort you out. I told you, I have the stuff for you. I'll do you a swap.'

The woman held out her hand again for her prescription, but he made no move to give it back.

'I said leave me alone,' she repeated, but this time, she didn't sound as sure about it.

'Go on then, do what you want,' he said. 'I'm only trying to help you. Don't come looking for me tomorrow when your teeth are going to fall out of your head with the pain, because that's what that other stuff is going to do to you.'

He offered her the prescription but she didn't take it back. She looked like she was worn out and not able to keep up the fight. He saw her starting to crack. 'You don't even need to pay me,' he explained, as if he was doing her a favour. 'We can do a swap. Go on, here, take this back. You go and pick it up from the chemist, and I'll meet you up there and sort you out with a couple of grams.'

He put the prescription back into her hand and jumped back on his bike, taking off in the direction of the flats before there could be any further discussion.

The woman looked after him for a moment as he cycled away and then picked up her shopping bag again, shuffling up the road in the direction of the chemist.

'That's messed up,' Kev said eventually as we walked home. I didn't ever want to go back to the Brickhouse after what we had seen. I couldn't stop thinking about that poor woman, how trapped she looked as the dealer finally broke her. She had gone there to get help, but if that was what she was up against, how could she ever hope to get better? How could anyone?

'Ah, jeez, Philly, I dunno,' Kev said when I didn't answer him. He knew what I was thinking. 'I only saw John with you a couple of weeks ago. He definitely wasn't as bad as that.'

Kev was right. He wasn't that bad. Not yet anyway.

10

For the next few weeks, training was crazy, which kept my mind off John. Or maybe it was crazy because I was trying to keep my mind off John. Either way, I was glad of it.

By the time Colm blew his whistle at the end of a session, every one of us was wrecked. He'd gather us around for one last chat before sending us home, and he'd be surrounded by T-shirts soaked through with sweat, red faces looking back at him and hands on heads as we tried to gulp down the air to catch our breath.

'Every single game, we talk about opportunities, don't we?' he reminded us one night after training. 'And we talk about making good decisions on the pitch in those moments, and how that's what helps us to keep getting better as a team.

'Not everyone here wants to get into the academy, I know that. It's a massive commitment. But for those of you who do,' he said, looking around the group, 'going to these trials is your opportunity. So make the good decisions and work hard for it. And if you don't get picked or it doesn't work out, don't worry. This is only the start – there'll be lots more opportunities, and at least you'll know you tried your best for this one. But don't let it pass you by.'

I could have kept training all through the night after listening to that.

Colm came over to me as I was tying the laces on my runners. 'Great stuff again tonight, Philly, well done,' he said, giving me a thumbs up. 'Keep it going now.'

We trained every day from that point on: me, Kev and three or four of the others. We were in Poppintree Park for our usual training with the rest of the team on Tuesdays and Thursdays, and we had our matches most Saturdays, but every other day, we'd meet up ourselves and throw down the cones and do our own sessions. We did the tackling drills that Colm liked; we practised one-on-ones under high balls; we had shooting sessions, free-taking competitions, anything we could think of until either we started getting called home or the sun went down, whichever was later.

We met in Albert College Park where a few of the Glasnevin lads, Taz and Jimmy and Liam, hung around. It was nearly as close for me and Kev as Poppintree Park was and, although I didn't say it, I was happy to get away from the blocks for a bit. Everything reminded me of John. I saw Aaron and a few of John's other friends one day, and Aaron called me over, but I didn't want to talk to them. It was their fault too. They were all fine, going off to work every morning or doing whatever, and they weren't addicted to heroin. Why didn't they help John or try to get him to stop? If I'd gone over to them when Aaron called, that's what I would have asked them, but I left it.

I kept thinking that I'd see John eventually, hoping that I would. I didn't want to talk to him either, but part of me still wanted to know that he was okay.

—

As the trials got closer, we trained even harder. One day, Taz and Liam were already waiting for us in the park, kicking a ball back and forth between themselves on one of the empty pitches.

'Did Jimmy not come up with you?' Kev asked as he took the cones out of my bag and started arranging them in two big squares of four each. Because we were by ourselves with no coach, whoever was ready first set up whatever they wanted for the first drill and we went from there.

'We knocked in for him on the way over,' Taz said. 'He said he'd follow us up. He was finishing off an essay that's due in tomorrow but he was nearly done. We'll start without him anyway – there's no point in waiting.'

We were halfway through our second drill when Jimmy arrived to join us. At the start of every season, a few lads left the team and a few new faces joined, but Jimmy had been there as long as I had, back since we started out at Under-7s. He was our centre-back, big and powerful but fast too. He was probably better going forward than he was when he was defending, but it meant we worked well together; he knew that if he pushed up a bit, I'd be there to mind the house behind him.

We loved playing together, mainly because we both felt like we could read what the other was thinking. That, and the fact that neither of us was afraid to get stuck in – the Bash Brothers, Colm liked to call us – but when it came to the trials, I had a feeling that the two of us were competing for one place. Colm hadn't exactly said that, but from listening to him at training, it sounded like he was thinking of sending one player from each line: a defender, a midfielder and a forward. If that turned out to be the case, and I was up against Jimmy, I had to be at my best.

We trained for an hour or more, and at the end of it, we finished off with a free-taking competition, which Kev won. It was Monday, which meant we only had two more sessions with the whole team before Colm picked his three for the trials. Looking at the work that the five of us had just put in, he was going to have an impossible job.

When we got back up the road home, I said goodbye to Kev and went up the stairwell into my block. Halfway up, I could hear the footsteps of someone coming down. It was dark, and all of the lights were broken as usual, so I hung back until I saw who it was. For a moment, my brain tricked me into hoping that it might even be John.

'Ah, Philly,' Mr O'Dea said with a smile, picking me out in the darkness as he came around the corner. He had no jacket on and the newspaper tucked under his arm. 'Good man yourself. I'm just going out for a stroll.'

I knew he was going to the pub – nobody goes for a walk at nine o'clock at night and brings the newspaper with them – but I said nothing. I had been worrying about bumping into the O'Deas or Mags Flynn or Claire Mac or any of the neighbours on the street, afraid they might say they hadn't seen John in a while and ask me where he was, if he was doing okay – or worse, the concern and the pity as they asked if I was doing okay, now that my brother had a heroin addiction. Did they even know anything about what was going on?

I was relieved when Mr O'Dea didn't ask. 'I heard there's trials for Dublin this weekend,' he said. 'I hope you get picked. I'm always telling Rita that you're a great little footballer and how you're going to be Ballymun's next star. The next Colm Doyle, I told her.'

My stomach did a little flip when he said that. Imagine.

'She's not really into the football, Rita, so she doesn't know who Colm Doyle is,' he said with a bit of a chuckle, 'but I'll tell you one thing, when it's you out there playing for the Dubs in a few years' time, she'll be your number one fan. You won't be able to get up or down these stairs,' he said, pointing at the filthy walls on either side of us, 'because there'll be bunting everywhere.'

'I hope so,' I said quietly.

'Get your hats, scarves and headbands,' he shouted, doing his best Dublin accent, and he started laughing. 'You never know, I might get myself a little stall and set it up out the front there. Anyway, Philly, I'm off for my walk.' He winked. 'Good luck at the weekend.'

—

Training was at seven o'clock on Thursday evening, but if you arrived on time, you were as good as late. By a quarter to seven, everyone was there, togged and ready to go.

'Right, lads, listen up,' Colm said, calling us all together. 'I know the plan was that I'd name the three players picked for the trials after training tonight, but there's been a change of plan.'

The giddiness vanished in an instant. I'd never heard us fall quiet so quickly.

'We have a match on Saturday, away to Kilmacud Crokes, and we've a few things I want to work on tonight before that. I want you listening to me, I want you focused, and I don't want you to be wondering if you're training well enough to get picked for the trials.'

He took a notebook out of his jacket pocket and opened it. 'Whatever happens tonight, I've already made my mind up, so I'm going to announce the names now and then we'll have our normal session.'

Taz gave me a dig in the ribs. Kev was over on the other side of the group, standing in between Jimmy and Liam. I caught his eye and he mouthed, 'Good luck.' I raised my eyebrows, wishing him the same.

'You haven't made this easy for me, lads,' Colm continued. 'You really haven't. I'll be honest, there are at least seven or eight of you that I'd be sending on Sunday if I was able to. But you know I can't.

'All I'm saying is that if you're not one of the three names written down here' – he tapped on the notebook with the top of his pencil – 'don't be too disappointed because, honestly, the gap between the three who made it and those who didn't is practically nothing. And there'll be other trials too; this is only the start of it, not the end. You just need to keep working as hard as you have done for the last three weeks and your chance will come again, I promise.'

I had already analysed everything that happened over the last few weeks to death, but as Colm spoke, I found myself doing it again. It was still too close to call, whatever he had decided.

'For the three of you who have been picked – lads, go out there with your heads held high. You're as good as any footballers in the city and deserve to be there as much as anyone else – more than some, I'd say. You're representing all of us, you're representing Ballymun. Go out there and do us proud.' He looked down at his notes. 'If I call your name, stand over here on the right behind me. Kev Considine …'

Kev clenched his fist and gave the air a little punch as he moved over to stand behind Colm. Everyone else clapped; the way Kev was playing, nobody would argue against him being picked.

'Taz O'Leary …'

I cheered when Taz's name was read out. 'Yeow, go on, Taz! Well done,' I said, and I gave him a slap on the top of the head in celebration.

'Watch it, mind the hair,' he said, jokingly pushing me away and pretending to fix it back into place. He was delighted.

'And Philly Caffrey.'

I was so busy messing that I nearly missed my own name. I hadn't time to worry about the fact that there was only one place left, and that only one out of me and Jimmy and Liam was going to make it. By the time my brain caught up with the real world and I realised any of those things, I was in. I had been picked for a trial with the Dublin academy.

Colm led the applause when the three names had been announced. 'Congratulations, lads, the very best of luck on Sunday. Everyone else, hard luck and well done. On the plus side,' he added, 'if everyone keeps training the way you've been training for the last few weeks, we're going to have some run when Féile comes around.'

That got a big cheer from the whole team. As I went to join Kev and Taz, I felt an arm around my shoulder. 'At least the Bash Brothers will be represented,' Jimmy said, giving me a bit of a shake. 'Well done, man, best of luck.'

Before I could even say thanks, Colm had put a bag of bibs down in the middle of the circle.

'Right, half with bibs, half without. Bibs down the far end, no bibs stay at this end. Let's go – we've a game on Saturday to think about.'

Kev grabbed three of the orange bibs from the bag and threw one each to me and Taz. The three of us jogged together down to the other goalmouth, where Colm already had a small area marked out with cones.

'Lads,' Taz said, bursting, 'we've trials for Dublin on Sunday.' Even as he said it, it didn't sound particularly real. I couldn't wait to get home and tell everyone – everyone except for the one person I should have been the most excited to tell. I still hadn't forgiven John for everything that had happened, but that didn't mean that I didn't miss him.

We split into four groups, a group in each corner, and while we waited for the drill to start, a few more of the lads came over to congratulate me. I tried to put it all out of my mind, to focus on training and on Saturday's match like Colm had said, but I was buzzing and I couldn't hide it. If this was how good it felt just getting picked to go for an academy trial, what would it be like to be a senior player running out in Croke Park, standing there in front of thousands of fans while the national anthem was played?

Colm blew his whistle and I snapped out of my dreams before the band got to the third line of 'Amhrán na bhFiann'. Kev went first, sprinting diagonally across the rectangle, popping up a handpass to Liam, who was coming towards him at full speed from the opposite corner, all the while making sure they didn't collide with the other two players running across their path doing the same thing. It was one of Colm's favourites for the start of a session, all about the three Cs – co-ordination, communication and concentration – and it made sure that everyone was switched on straight away.

I was determined to train as if my place in the trials depended on it. Taz was opposite me when I got to the top of the line. I waited for him to move and, once he did, I went off at full speed. I was concentrating on his run, but out of the corner of my eye, I could see the others coming too. The four of us were all going to get there at the exact same time. We were going to run straight into each other.

Taz saw it too and slowed down to delay for half a second, avoiding the crash, but as he passed to me, he under-hit it and the ball was slightly too low for me to catch. I should have left it, let it hit the ground, and started again, but without even thinking, I stretched out my left foot to try to get my boot underneath it and keep it alive.

The pain that ripped through the back of my leg felt like someone had slashed me with a hot knife. I let out a yelp as I pulled up sharply, managing to hobble two more steps on my good leg before I let myself fall to the ground.

Everyone stopped. Martin, our goalkeeper, was the closest person to me. 'Are you all right, Philly? What is it?'

'My hamstring,' I said, gritting my teeth to distract myself from the pain. 'It's gone.'

11

Martin reached out his hand to help me back to my feet, but as soon as I tried to put weight on my leg, it was as if the invisible hand holding the knife had pushed it in even deeper and then twisted it. I couldn't stand, never mind walk or run, and Martin and Kev took one side each and slowly helped me over to the sideline.

Colm hadn't seen me get hurt. He had been working with the other group when he noticed that our drill had stopped and saw the two lads propping me up. He came over immediately to see if I was okay.

'I'm grand, I'm grand,' I reassured him, worried that my face might be telling a different story. 'My hamstring just felt a bit tight there when I was reaching for the ball. I just need a minute to stretch it out and I'll be able to run it off.'

Colm didn't believe a word of it. 'If it was only a bit of tightness, you'd have been able to walk over by yourself,' he said, looking at Martin and Kev for confirmation.

'They were just making sure,' I said.

'Fair enough,' he said. 'But still, it's not a hundred per cent so don't take any chances with it. Sit the rest of the evening out. I'm not having you rushing back and then making it worse.'

Colm was right, and in any other situation, I would have agreed – reluctantly – and done what I was told. Being injured wasn't an option, though. Nobody needed to say it, but if I wasn't fit enough to finish training, I wasn't fit enough to go to the trials on Sunday. I had to try to keep going.

'It already feels better,' I lied, ignoring Colm's instruction as I forced myself to jog back towards the rest of the group. I faced away from him so he couldn't see me grimace. 'If it gets any worse, or I can't run it off in the next few minutes, I'll stop.' Another lie; I'd have tried to keep training with a broken leg if I thought it would get me a place on the trials.

'Don't do anything stupid,' Colm shouted after me. He knew me long enough to know there was no point arguing when I was in this kind of mood. The best he could do was hope that I eventually saw a bit of sense myself.

I took my place as the whistle went and the next drill started, digging the tips of my fingers into the muscle while I waited to try to massage it back to normal. I convinced myself that it was already getting better, that it was only a pull, or maybe a slight strain if I was really lucky. But as soon I got to the top of the line and I tried to sprint, the pain sizzled through my leg again. I couldn't do it. I dropped the ball and limped back to the sideline, blinking away the tears and hoping that nobody saw them.

If anyone asked if I was crying, I'd tell them it was from the pain. A lot of other players were disappointed they hadn't been picked for the trials, and they all managed to keep it together and not let it show. Now it was my turn to do the same.

I sat on my gear bag for the best part of an hour and watched the rest of the session, passes zipping back and forth, tackles flying, and everyone looking like they were having incredible fun.

'Would you not have got back into your tracksuit?' Kev asked when training had finished for the evening and everyone was getting changed.

'Huh?'

'You look frozen sitting there,' he said.

I was shivering, and I had been in such a daze that I hadn't even noticed. I wrestled my boots off without untying the laces and put my jumper on. Then Colm called me.

'I need a quick word with you before you go, please,' he said. My stomach dropped. 'You too, please, Jimmy. Just hang on there for two minutes while I'm chatting to Philly and I'll be with you then.'

Colm walked a little bit away from where the rest of the team were changing so they couldn't hear our conversation. 'How is it feeling now?' he asked me.

'Yeah, it's grand. It actually doesn't hurt at all now,' I said, which was the truth. 'You're right, I was better off not training tonight. I'll just rest it again tomorrow and I'll be grand then for the weekend.'

'I think it might take a bit longer than that,' Colm said, puncturing my optimism. I knew what was coming next. 'I can't send you to the trials if you're injured, Philly. It's not fair on the other lads. I need to make a decision tonight, and tonight, you can't even jog, never mind do a full day of drills and matches.'

I couldn't even look him in the eye. 'Can you just wait until the morning and we'll see how it is then?' I asked, but Colm shook his head.

'Jimmy will go on Sunday instead of you,' he said.

'I'm sorry, I know how disappointing this is.'

The rest of the team had started to drift off home, one by one, but there were still a few left. Jimmy and Kev were looking over in our direction, although they hardly needed to be lip-readers to figure out what was going on.

'Look, this won't make it any easier for you,' Colm said, 'and please don't go saying this, but you were the first name on my list coming down here tonight. You've been excellent all season, and you've been training and playing out of your skin for the last few weeks.'

I tried one last time to change his mind. Getting picked for the trials was the only thing that mattered to me right now. I had been so determined, I had been working so hard, that I had barely had time to be worrying about John and everything else that was going on. I was so excited to go home with some good news for Mam and Dad. I had to go on Sunday. I needed this.

'I'll be fine in a few days, I will,' I promised, my voice cracking, but it was clear that Colm had made his decision.

'I hope so,' he said. 'Go on, you better go straight home. Try to take it easy for a bit, will you?'

And that was it.

—

Kellie was in the sitting room when I got home, sitting on the couch by herself, working on a drawing in her notebook. 'What are you up to?' she said suspiciously when she heard me come in and go straight to the freezer.

I took a tea-towel from the countertop and emptied a tray of ice cubes into it, and then tried to wrap it into a makeshift bandage around the back of my hamstring. A few of the ice cubes fell out onto the kitchen floor, and they stuck to my fingers as I picked them up.

'Here, Frosty the Snowman, give up the messing,' Kellie warned as she came in to see what the fuss was about. 'Mam and Dad will kill you if they come home and find puddles of water all over the place.'

'Do I look like I'm messing?' I growled, and she knew straight away that I was upset.

She picked up the last two ice cubes that had scattered out into the hall and handed them back to me. 'What are you after doing to yourself now?'

A couple of bits of ice escaped on me again, slipping out the sides as I fumbled with the knot, and I flung the whole lot, tea-towel and all, into the sink in frustration.

'Stop,' she said, concerned, rearranging the ice neatly into a far better bandage than I had managed. 'Come here, gimme a look and I'll do it properly for you.'

I limped over and she tied the tea-towel tight to my leg. The cold pressed through onto my skin and it already felt good.

'How long do you have to do this for?' she asked.

'Until it's better. I got picked for the trials on Sunday, but I can't go if I'm like this.'

'Don't worry, we'll have it sorted by Sunday,' she reassured me. She picked up the empty ice tray from the counter and ran it under the cold tap to fill it again, then put it back into the freezer. 'There's another tray of cubes already in there. Come back in to me in twenty minutes and we'll put a fresh one on then.'

I kept ice on it for the night, with Kellie's help, and I did the same again the next morning before I went to school. The tea-towel we had used was still soaking wet, so I wrung it out into the sink and filled it again before sitting down to have my breakfast.

I went into the bathroom before I got dressed and locked the door behind me. I quietly reached up and opened the little glass cabinet where Mam and Dad kept any of their medicine. It looked empty. Normally, there'd be a few little brown plastic tubs of pills, leftovers from the last time someone was sick or put away for the next time, but they were all gone. A thought of John flashed into my head, locked in the bathroom just like I was now, desperate for whatever he could get his hands on. I shook it aside quickly; for all I knew, Mam and Dad had got there before him and moved their medicine to hide it from him.

The bare shelves made it easy to find what I was looking for: a tiny jar with an orange and blue label and a picture of a mean-looking tiger snarling at me on the front of it. This was the stuff I had seen Dad use whenever he came in from work and had a sore back. I wasn't sure what exactly it was supposed to do, but it couldn't hurt to try.

I scooped out a big glob from what was left in the jar and gave it a sniff. It was a really powerful smell, a bit like one of those strong chewing gums that were supposed to be good for you when you had a cold. The hairs on the inside of my nose felt like somebody had put a lit match to them, and my eyes started to water. Whatever this stuff was, it must be good.

I rubbed the ointment into the back of my leg. It was hot, very hot, which made me panic. I hadn't read the instructions to see how much I was supposed to use. What if I had put too much on and burned all the skin off my leg? I waited until the heat level went from roasting to just nicely warm, and then I washed my hands quickly before I touched any other part of my body and accidentally set it on fire too. I closed the medicine cabinet but I didn't put the jar back in; nobody would miss it if I brought it to school with me. And then I flushed the toilet – just in case anyone was wondering what I had been up to – and went to get ready.

During geography class I asked Ms Breen if I could go to the toilet, and in the cubicle, I quickly rubbed a fresh layer of the tiger ointment into my leg. The smell of it followed me back up the corridor and, as I sat back down at my desk, I was afraid one of the other lads would put up their hand and tell Ms Breen there was a funny smell, and I'd be caught. But nobody said anything.

I didn't go out at all that evening, even though it was Friday; I stayed in to put more ice on my leg instead. June and Lindy had knocked up for dinner, and they were sitting inside having a glass of wine with Mam.

'Look at you,' Lindy said with surprise, watching me tie up another tea-towel bandage. I would have asked Kellie to do it for me again but she gone up to the youth club in the White Elephant with her friends. I had been paying very close attention after making a mess of my first attempt.

'I never knew you were a doctor. Have you anything there for a sore neck?' June laughed. 'I must have slept on it funny last night.'

The next morning, I put my Kickhams tracksuit on and packed my boots and the rest of my kit into my bag as normal, and I was ready to go when Kev called over for me.

'Where are you going with the bag?' he asked, raising his eyebrows. 'You off out to the supermarket or something?'

'Ah, you know, just in case …'

'Just in case? You're a headcase, you are,' he said, getting more high-pitched. 'You're not seriously thinking of playing, are you?'

I shrugged my shoulders. 'Nah, there's no chance that Colm will let me. It does feel much better, though – honestly,' I insisted, but one look at Kev told me that even he wasn't buying that story.

We all met up outside the shops on the Ballymun Road, and then we piled onto the minibus to go to the southside, to Stillorgan, where Kilmacud Crokes' pitches were. When we stopped at a set of lights, I chanced my arm and moved into the empty seat beside Colm.

'I think I'm probably okay to be a sub,' I suggested. 'You could bring me on a few minutes at the end and see what you think?'

'No, not today, it's too much of a risk,' he said firmly, making it clear there was no point in me even asking again. While everyone else got togged for the match and did their stretches, I took three balls out of the bag and went down to help Martin warm up in goal. I threw a few balls in to him to start, letting him come and catch them high in the air, and then I kicked a few, first off my right and then off my left. My leg felt good, which, when I thought about it, only made me feel worse.

It was a tight game but we won by two points. We

were one up and hanging on a bit as Crokes pressed hard for an equaliser in the final seconds, but Jimmy somehow got his hand in to knock the ball away from one of their forwards and we came down the other end and scored to make sure of the win. It was another big result, not only because it kept us on top of the league for now, but also with one eye on Féile, where Crokes were surely going to be another one of our big rivals in Dublin.

Kev's mam and dad were gone out for the afternoon, so when the minibus dropped us all back off at the shops again, he came home with me.

'We're home, we won again,' I called out as we came in, but nobody answered, and when I opened the door to the sitting room to see if anybody was home, a third person was there with Mam and Dad.

'Howaya, Philly,' John said.

12

I looked from John to Mam and Dad, and then back to John again. 'You're home?' I said, but it barely came out as a whisper.

'Ah, yeah, I missed you all too much,' he said. 'Howaya Kev.'

'All right, John,' Kev said, still standing behind me, unsure what he should do now. 'I better go and check if anyone's home,' he said quickly, to nobody in particular, turning back towards the front door. 'I'll talk to you later on.'

He closed both doors gently behind him as he left. Nobody said anything for a moment. John was pale. His skin looked like paper, like it would tear as soon you touched it, and big red blotches were dotted around his face. He'd taken off his baseball cap and put it on the table, and his hair was stuck to the top of his head; it was a lot longer than usual. I tried to remember how he had looked five weeks ago, the last time that I saw him, but I couldn't get past how sick he seemed right now.

'Mam and Dad said they told you and Kellie the whole story,' John said when he spoke eventually. 'I'm sorry, Philly.'

He waited for me to respond and when I didn't, he continued. 'I'm trying to get better,' he said, and I could hear in his voice that he really meant it. 'I am. It's just hard.'

'Where have you been?' I asked.

'Ah, you know, here and there,' he said. 'I have a few friends in town that I was able to crash with for a while.'

'Are you back for good this time?'

Dad shifted uneasily in his chair.

'I hope so, yeah,' John said, and slowly pulled himself up out of the couch. He moved like an old man, like every bone in his body ached. 'Anyway, come here and give us a hug, would you? I haven't seen you in weeks.'

I was happy to see that he was home and safe, but I didn't want a hug. I didn't know what I wanted. 'I've to go and sort my gear out,' I said and I turned my back on him, leaving him standing there waiting, his arms hanging by his sides.

John's bags were lying in the middle of our bedroom floor where he had dropped them, open and waiting to be unpacked. Some of the stuff smelled like it hadn't been properly washed since he left. I pushed the bags out of the way with my foot and climbed up the ladder onto my bed. I thought Mam or Dad might come in to check on me and see if I was okay, but nobody did. I pulled my knees in to my chest and lay there, staring at the wall, trying not to think. I could hear them talking again in the sitting room, and I heard the front door open when Kellie came home, and then I fell asleep and didn't wake up again until I was called for dinner.

—

Dinner was fish and chips, our usual Saturday treat from Macari's. The salt and vinegar hit me before Dad had even started to dish it out from the brown paper bags, and I could hear my stomach rumbling. I was starving.

Dad handed out each of the five plates, saving the one with the biggest piece of fish for Mam. Dad had done that for as long as I could remember. Even when we were all a lot younger, pushing and elbowing for a bit of space as we all squeezed in together to eat, Dad would always save the best for Mam and make a big show out of making sure that she got her food before any of the rest of us did. Sometimes he'd sing a little bit of a song as he gave her her food, in a jokey way – like the old Elvis one that he liked, 'I Can't Help Falling in Love with You' – and Mam would roll her eyes at him and say, 'What are you like?' But we could all see that she was smiling.

Those days felt like a long time ago now.

I tapped the bottom of the ketchup bottle until there was a little pool on the side of my plate, then I passed it to Kellie, who did the same. For a minute, the only sound was of our knives and our forks as they scraped the plates and the golden crunch of the batter as the fish fell apart into little pieces.

'You never told us how your match went, Philly?' Dad said.

'Good, yeah,' I said. 'We won by two points.'

He looked at me hopefully, waiting to hear a little bit more than the bare minimum, but I didn't really feel like talking.

Mam tried again. 'How's your leg today?'

'Yeah, it feels a good bit better,' I said, and dipped another chip into the ketchup. I just wanted to be left alone.

I loved dinner time; it was the only time that we all spent together, really, and it was usually a battle to get a word in edgeways. Everyone wanted to be first, or next, with their story. There was always a tale to tell, whether it was something that had happened in school or in work, or a bit of news that Mam and Dad had heard from one of the neighbours.

But now there was only one thing that mattered, and it was the one thing that nobody wanted to talk about. Everything else seemed irrelevant. Whenever someone spoke, it sounded forced, and every new conversation quickly died after a few short sentences. By trying so hard for things to be normal, they only became more strange.

John put his fork down on the side of his plate while he finished chewing the food in his mouth. 'I have a funny one for you,' he said, and he launched into a story about some guy called Stephen that I didn't know. It was about how some people had mistaken this Stephen lad for a famous American actor, and how he started posing for photographs and signing autographs, and then the newspaper wanted to send someone down to interview him … I don't know what the story was about, really. I was too angry with John to listen properly.

John kept going and I kept getting angrier. I stared at him, hoping he'd see that I didn't find it funny, but he was too caught up in the story to even notice me. I could feel my face getting hot. Why was he acting like nothing was wrong, like everything was normal? I wanted to scream at him: this isn't normal; normal people don't joke around like a heroin addiction is no big deal. Our family isn't normal any more. And it's all your fault.

John was up off the couch now, acting out every bit of it, trying to stop laughing at his own story for long enough to finish actually telling it. Mam and Dad were doing their best to smile along but I couldn't sit there any longer. I stood up quickly to leave, accidentally knocking my glass off the arm of the chair where I had left it. It was empty but it shattered as it hit the floor, scattering jagged bits of glass around everyone's feet.

'I'm going out for a while,' I announced, scooping up the big bits of glass nearest to me and squeezing past Kellie before anyone could try to stop me.

'You haven't even finished your dinner,' Mam said, motioning for me to sit back down.

'It's grand, I'm not hungry anyway.'

I had interrupted John mid-sentence. He sat back down without finishing his story, his shoulders slumping as he picked a few mushy peas off his plate with his fingers. 'Don't be like that, Philly, come on,' he said without looking up. 'It's just a story. You don't need to go, I'll shut up now.'

But I couldn't stay. I needed fresh air, and I needed to get away from that table. Everybody else might have been happy to pretend that our lives were grand, but I wasn't. If John had any idea how much he was hurting Mam and Dad, how worried they were because of him, he wouldn't be pretending either.

—

The evening breeze slapped me in the face as I crossed the field. I thought about calling to Kev's, even though I had no real reason to, but then I changed my mind. I wandered aimlessly instead, and before I knew it, I was standing outside Colm's front door, waiting for him to answer.

'Philly.' He sounded surprised. 'I wasn't expecting to see you again this evening. Is everything all right?'

'No, not really, to be honest. Can I talk to you for a minute?'

'Sure, come in.'

I wondered if I should take my shoes off as I stepped into the hall. Everything about Colm's house was always so spotless. He closed the door to the front room so that the noise from the television wasn't too loud. It sounded like he was watching a match.

I got straight to the point. 'You need to let me go to the trials tomorrow. I can't miss them.'

I knew I was wasting my time asking again, and I expected Colm to be mad at me for barging into his house unannounced on a Saturday night to waste his too.

'It's not about me letting you go or not.' He sighed. 'I picked you to go. You absolutely deserve to go, fair and square. But you're not fit.'

'I am.'

Colm scrunched up his face like it was physically paining him to have this argument all over again.

'Okay, I'm not fully fit,' I admitted, 'but I'm still fit enough to go there and be good enough. You have to let me go. I'm begging you, please.'

'What's going on?' He sounded concerned.

I wanted to tell him. I wanted to tell him the whole story – about John, about how I needed this opportunity to take over every minute of my life so I wouldn't have time to think about anything else – but I just couldn't do it. I couldn't admit what was wrong. I didn't want Colm to know that John had a drug addiction, for him to think that my brother was just another Ballymun zombie, strung out on the blocks. He'd never look at me in the same way if he knew.

'It's my dream,' I pleaded with him. 'It's the only thing I want. And if I can stand, I can do enough to get into the academy. Please.'

'Are you sure that everything's okay, Philly?' Colm asked, the wrinkles on his forehead getting deeper. 'Did something happen at home?'

Yes, I wanted to say. Yes, something terrible is happening at home. But I shook my head. 'No, nothing like that. You just need to let me go tomorrow.'

Colm's face fell, and he rubbed his chin with the palm of his hand. 'I wish I could, Philly, but there's nothing I can do, I'm sorry. I've already given Gerry Mangan the names, and Jimmy is going with Kev and Taz in the morning. I'm sorry.'

I knew Colm would move heaven and earth for me – for any of us on that team. He had done it so many times over the years. And I knew by him, by his apologies, that there was nothing more he could do now. He gave me a pat on the shoulder as he went to open the door and show me out. 'There'll be other opportunities, don't worry,' he reassured me.

'Ring him again,' I said.

'What?' Colm was a bit taken aback.

'You could ring Gerry again,' I said. 'Explain what happened. Tell him that I was picked originally, and that I picked up a knock but that I'm fit now, and ask him if I can go as well as the lads.'

Colm thought about it for a moment, and then shook his head. 'They're very strict on the numbers,' he said. 'It's three per club max.'

'Can you please just ring him and explain and double-check?' I persisted. 'Please.'

'Okay, okay,' he said finally. 'But please don't get your hopes up. I really don't think this is going to work.'

He took his phone out of his pocket and started dialling as he went into another room. I could hear him talking, so at least Gerry had answered the phone, but the words were muffled. I couldn't make out what Colm was saying or what kind of reaction his suggestion was getting.

I thought about opening the door into the front room to see what match was on the TV, but I distracted myself instead with the painting hanging in the hall, trying to feel the power of the sea as it crashed against the cliff face. Colm was still on the phone. It seemed to go on for ages.

'Okay, I'll tell him that, Gerry,' he said as he came back out to me. 'Thanks very much for taking the call. I'll chat to you soon. Go on. Bye. Bye. Bye.'

He hung up the phone but it was hard to tell whether it had gone well or not. The look on his face wasn't happy or sad. 'Gerry Mangan said to make sure your boots are spotless in the morning,' he said, breaking into a smile. 'You're in.'

13

The next morning I cut a long strip from the roll of bandage and wrapped it around and around my leg until it was tight. I taped it up at the edges to hold it in place and looked at myself in the mirror. There was no hiding the fact that my leg was strapped up, but other than that, I was ready to go.

Mam was in her room. It was her Sunday to work and she was getting ready to leave. She yawned as she packed her bag, rubbing at the dark circles under her eyes. I heard her get up sometimes in the middle of the night and go into the kitchen. She'd close the door behind her so as not to disturb any of the rest of us, but I could still hear the kettle boiling and the click of the switch to announce that it was done. I wondered if she had slept at all last night or if she had been up all night worrying.

Dad was gone since before I had even woken up. 'They're bringing everyone in,' he explained to me when I came back home the night before. 'We've to be off site by the end of the day on Friday, so it's all hands on deck between now and then.'

I had raced back from Colm's, completely forgetting about John for a moment, excited to tell them the good news that I was going to the trials after all. Dad could see how disappointed I was that he wouldn't be able to come with me – that neither of them would. One of them always came to my matches, if not both of them. It would be strange not to have them there with me.

'Good luck today,' Mam said, kissing me on the forehead. 'I know you won't need luck, but it couldn't hurt to have a bit anyway.' She wrapped me up in a big hug and I could smell the perfume on her blouse. 'You're a great kid, Philip,' she said, squeezing me tight. 'We're going to be okay, you hear me? We'll pull through this.' I thought of John and wondered where he was.

Kev and his mam, Trish, were waiting outside for me, and I threw my bag into the boot and jumped into the back seat of their green Ford Fiesta.

'You both sure you've got everything?' Trish asked before she started the car. The clock on the dashboard said 10.05 so we had plenty of time, but we didn't want to realise we'd forgotten something and then have to turn back in a panic. I got out to check my bag again, even though I'd already double-checked it before I left the flat, and Kev did the same. It was better to be safe than sorry.

There wasn't much traffic at that hour of the morning, so the drive to St Anne's Park in Raheny took about twenty minutes. Trish found a parking spot and the three of us walked through the park to the pitches where the trials were being held. Taz and his dad were already there by the time we arrived, and Jimmy and his dad and his brother were a minute or two behind us.

'I thought you weren't coming?' Taz said. He and Jimmy were both a bit surprised to see me.

'And they didn't mind Colm sending four of us?' Jimmy asked when I explained what had happened. He seemed worried that we had already done something wrong, and that one of us was going to be sent home before the trials even started.

'No, Colm said it's all grand,' I reassured him. 'He was on the phone to Gerry Mangan for ages last night, and Gerry said there had been a few other injuries, so they must have a bit of extra space.'

I had never met Gerry Mangan before but I knew what he looked like, and I could see him in the distance. Three other coaches were with him, all dressed in Dublin tracksuits, two setting out cones in a series of precise patterns while the other followed behind them with a bag full of footballs.

As it got closer to eleven o'clock, more and more players arrived and started to cluster together in groups of two and three, looking for the familiar faces of their teammates, while we all waited for things to get started. If this had been a normal training session up in Poppintree Park, someone would have taken a ball out of the bag and started a kickabout, but nobody wanted to move a muscle until we were told to do otherwise by the coaches.

'Don't worry about being a team player today – are you listening to me? These aren't your teammates yet.'

The voice caught my attention straight away and I turned to see who it was. Near us were two blond brothers, standing by themselves. I recognised them both immediately: Mick Devanney, wearing his Dublin tracksuit, doing all the talking, Andrew listening carefully as he stretched and warmed up beside him.

'The ones who stand out are the ones who are going to get picked, I'm telling you,' Mick said as I kept listening. He was slapping his hands together at the end of every sentence, making his own sound effects. 'The first chance you get to make a big hit, you make it. If your team gets a free, you take it. And if you get a chance to shoot, don't think about anything except putting it straight over the bar, okay? Nobody here is going to remember the player who made the pass. They're all looking to see who kicked the score.'

If Colm had been there, I was pretty sure he'd be telling us the exact opposite of that, which made me think that it was terrible advice. Part of me wished John had come with me too; he wouldn't have been much use when it came to advice on football, but I'd love to have heard the slagging he'd have given the two boys for being such posers. I turned to get Kev so he could listen for himself, but before I could do that, Gerry Mangan called everyone together.

He introduced himself and the three other coaches standing with him. Then he explained that the day would be divided up with two sessions in the morning, a short break for lunch and another session in the afternoon. He looked down at the sheet of paper on the clipboard in his hand. 'There are forty-three of you here today,' he said. 'We picked twenty players from last week's trial, and we'll be picking another twenty today, and that will be our forty players for this year's academy.

'And I should say,' he continued, 'it's wonderful to see some of our former academy graduates back here today as well: Mick, very best of luck with the seniors this summer.'

'Thanks, Gerry,' Mick Devanney said, turning to wave to everyone as if he was the President of Ireland.

'Okay so,' Gerry said, 'before we get going properly, if I call your name, come up to the front here, please.' He started to read from his list. 'David Creedon, Eamonn Power, Pádraig Byrne, and …'

As each name was called, a player moved out of the group and walked over to where the coaches were standing. Gerry ran his pen down the side of the page as he read and then flipped over to the second page, but he didn't call anybody else. He flipped back again to the first page and then stopped, looking puzzled.

'And …' he said again, pausing. 'Sorry now, I can't find the name. There's a lad here from Ballymun Kickhams that I was speaking to Colm Doyle about last night?'

I put my hand up as if I knew the answer to a question in school and stepped forward.

'Very good, thanks,' Gerry said. 'Sorry, you'll have to give me your name again. I must have lost the piece of paper where I wrote it down.'

'Philly McMahon.'

I spoke without thinking and I nearly surprised myself with the answer. I never used Dad's surname – I had always been Philly Caffrey, for everything – but something subconsciously made me say McMahon. I didn't want anyone to hear the name Caffrey and somehow make the connection that I was John's brother.

Gerry looked even more confused as he finally found my name on the list. 'McMahon? I have you down here as Philly Caffrey.'

'Yeah, that's me,' I said confidently. Backtracking now would only make things more awkward. 'That's my name on my birth cert, but I go by Philly McMahon normally if you want to change it.'

I waited while Gerry scribbled the correction onto his page.

'Right then, Philly,' he said. He spotted the bandage as he looked me up and down. 'You're fit, are you?'

'Yeah, I'm grand, it wasn't serious,' I said, turning away slightly so that the strapping wasn't so obvious.

'That's good. You won't mind doing a quick fitness test so.'

I wasn't sure if he was joking or not. Colm hadn't mentioned anything about a fitness test.

'You're not the only one, don't worry,' he said, seeing the stunned look on my face. He turned to speak to me and the three others together as a group. 'I'm sure the four of you know now why you've been picked out. We appreciate you letting us know that you're carrying knocks, but if you're not fit, there's not much point in you being here today, unfortunately.'

He pointed to the far touchline. 'We don't have time to be messing around,' he said. 'You're going to line up over there and do one sprint, the full width of the pitch. I'll be over there' – he pointed to the other touchline – 'with the watch. If you do it in under fifteen seconds, you can stay. If you're slower than that, you're going home. Does everyone understand?'

'Yes,' the four of us said together. We sounded like parrots.

'Wait for my whistle,' Gerry said. 'Get set on my first one, go on my second one. Good luck.'

We sometimes did sprints in training, and while I wasn't the fastest, I was always in the first six or seven. Fifteen seconds for the full width of the pitch was no warm-up jog, though. It was a flat-out sprint.

The four of us walked together over to our start line. We were racing the clock, not each other, but nobody felt like talking. Nerves, probably. My bandage was a giveaway but none of the others had anything obvious wrong with them.

Everyone else had fanned out in a line in front of the goal to watch us, and I could see Kev and Taz and Jimmy at the far end, closest to the finish line. I stood on the outside of the group when we got down to the start. Not that it really mattered, but I wanted to be able to keep an eye on the others without having to turn my head from side to side.

I quickly stretched my leg out again while we waited for Gerry to blow his whistle. I had been stretching and warming up since I'd got out of bed, and I was confident I could get through the day without any problems. But I didn't know what it was like going at full tilt in a sprint yet, and that unknown needled away at the back of my mind.

Gerry blew his first whistle and the four us crouched over the start line, the tips of our boots in a row, brushing up against the white of the pitch marking. When he blew his whistle again, I took off as hard as I could. There was no point in worrying about my leg any more. If something happened, or if it started to hurt, there'd be plenty of time to worry about it then.

The four of us were practically in a straight line, with nothing to choose between us. I was going as fast as I could but I had no idea if it was fast enough. We were halfway there. I expected cheering, that everyone watching would be willing us on, but there was near silence except for the sound of our boots chewing up the ground and the four of us trying to fill our lungs to keep going.

'Go on, Philly, push it.' Kev roared some encouragement.

I could see Gerry, one eye on us and one eye on the watch, ready to stop it as we crossed the line. We were nearly there. Just a few more strides. If I didn't make it now, it was over.

I hit the line and with my final stride I dipped like the sprinters do on the telly. I dipped so much that I nearly lost my balance and I started to stumble. I looked across the line – I was first, and the others were just behind me. There were only two of them, though, and when I looked back out into the middle of the field, the third – Eamonn, I think – was sitting down, holding his ankle.

'Well done, lads,' I said to the others in between breaths. Gerry had gone off to one side and was deep in conversation with the other coaches, so we still didn't know if the three of us were fast enough, or if any of us were.

'Pádraig, David,' he said as he walked back over to us. 'I'm very sorry, lads. You were just outside the time. We'll get you back down the next time and hopefully you'll be fully fit. Philly …'

He held the stopwatch out so I could read the time for myself: 14.81 seconds.

'Go get some water and catch your breath,' he said. 'We'll be starting in five minutes.'

14

By the time it was all over a few hours later, I wasn't sure if I had done enough to get through.

For the first two sessions before lunch, we were split up by position, and each of the coaches took one group: goalkeepers, defenders, midfielders and forwards. It was warm, even though there wasn't an inch in the clouds for the sun to shine through, and I certainly wasn't going to be the one to ask if we were allowed a break between drills. By the time we finished our first set of one-on-one work, my jersey was starting to change colour as the sweat seeped through in a ring below my neck. My leg felt fine, thankfully, because it was clear that this was going to be survival of the fittest.

When we switched to some two-on-two exercises, I was paired up with Jimmy. We were told to stay inside a small square, up against two other lads, and the aim was to keep possession for as long as possible; if we lost it, we had to try and get it back. Of all the pairs, Jimmy and I were the best at that drill. Even when we started without the ball, we won it back quickly and kept it until Conor, the coach who was working with us, called stop.

I watched Conor when the other pairs were working. He was taking a lot of notes, writing so frantically that I wondered how he could be doing that and watching what was happening at the same time. Every so often, he'd stop the drill and make us freeze on the spot in a specific position, and he'd pick out one player to ask why they had just made a certain choice. He never agreed or disagreed with the explanation – he just listened and then wrote more notes – but I thought about what Colm had told us over and over again: that playing well was mainly about making the right decision at the right time.

After lunch, the coaches split us into two bigger groups and set up two pitches for us to play 10-a-side matches. They put me and Jimmy on the same team again – maybe that was one of the things Conor had written in his notes – and when the two teams lined up, Andrew Devanney jogged down towards us. I expected that I'd be the one marking him, as usual, but he stayed out in the half-forward line and Jimmy picked him up instead.

Those heavy grey clouds gradually got darker and darker and then, in an instant, burst into a summer downpour just before the ball was thrown in. I went out to Jimmy and told him about the advice that Mick had given Andrew that morning.

'He's going to be a glory hunter today,' I said, trying to wipe my gloves dry on the front of my jersey. 'Don't worry about leaving space if you have to push up a bit to close him down. He's never going to pass it, and if he does, I'll be ready to cover in behind you.'

Andrew had been strutting around all morning as if he owned the place. He kept calling the coaches by their first names, and at one point, I'm pretty sure I heard him telling them there was a better way to set up one of the drills. Mick was at it too, standing over the coaches' shoulders, yapping away in their ears the whole time. I was getting irritated just watching the two of them and how they were behaving. They clearly thought they were better than the rest of us. If I couldn't be the one to mark Andrew out of the game, I wanted Jimmy to do it – and he did.

I played well too. The lad that I was marking was from Naomh Mearnóg out in Portmarnock, a good footballer, the kind of forward who would be slippery enough even on a dry day, and he got away from me twice for two good scores. I did everything right, pushed him well wide both times, thinking I'd done more than enough, and twice he managed to squeeze the ball over from impossible angles.

I was still thinking about his scores, replaying them in my mind, as we shook hands and walked off the pitch afterwards. Was that really what it was going to come down to? That, by the luck of the draw, I ended up marking the best forward on the pitch, and even though I'd kept him quiet for most of the game, he'd kicked two ridiculous points off me, and that was what the coaches would have noticed? Would that be the difference between me getting a place and not getting one?

'Well done, everyone,' Gerry Mangan said as we all gathered into a group at the end.

The rain had stopped but I could feel it in the bottom of my boots, and my socks were wringing wet.

'We expected a very high standard here today, and we certainly got it. Myself and the other coaches will need a little bit of time to think before we pick our final twenty. If you've made it, your club manager will be in touch with you tomorrow to give you the rest of the details. And if not, well done, and we'll hopefully see you again soon.'

—

I couldn't concentrate at all in school the next day. I sat at my desk in Mr Clark's maths class staring at the door, waiting for a knock. I was hoping Colm would call to the school to tell me I had been picked: that way everyone would know. I focused all my energy into imagining that somebody was about to knock on the door, in case it turned out that I was psychic and I could make it happen. But Colm didn't knock, and neither did anyone else.

The chalk in Mr Clark's hand squeaked across the blackboard. Two or three of the lads started howling, pressing their hands over their ears, and more joined in. We never missed a chance for a bit of messing.

'Sir, my ears. I think I'm gone deaf, sir!' Luke Nolan stood up from his desk and was making funny faces, like he was dizzy and the room was turning upside down on him.

'Quiet!' Mr Clark slammed his hand on the board with a crack. 'Luke, into your seat now.'

When we came back in after lunch, Colm still hadn't knocked. The longer the day went on, as we sat through our afternoon classes, I began to think that maybe he wouldn't. Your club manager will be in touch *if* you have been picked – that's what Gerry Mangan said. Maybe they had already contacted the 20 players who had been picked and told them. The more I thought about it, the more distracted I got.

When the bell went at the end of the day, everyone else went home and soon it was only me and Kev hanging around the yard by ourselves. It was my idea to stay, just in case Colm had planned to catch us at the end of the day but had got delayed for some reason.

'Maybe they still haven't made up their minds yet,' Kev suggested.

I looked at my watch. It was five past four, which meant that we'd been waiting for over half an hour. Colm wasn't coming. 'Come on and we'll go,' I said reluctantly.

But we didn't know where to go. Neither of us wanted to go home and wait there thinking about it until it got so late that we had no choice other than to accept that we hadn't been picked.

When we got to Kev's block, he went upstairs and reappeared a minute later, throwing me a football. 'Will we go down towards Albert College?' he suggested. 'Taz and Jimmy might be there, and if not, we can walk over towards their houses to see if they're hanging around. They might have heard from Colm.'

But when we got to the park, there was no sign of them, and we just stayed there instead, walking, talking and kicking the ball.

'Why did you change your name yesterday?' Kev asked.

I could have tried to brush him off but I wanted to talk. 'Did you not feel like a bit of an outsider there?'

'What do you mean?'

'The usual stuff. People hear that you're the lads from Ballymun, and they don't know anything about us, but they still think we're all poor, and that nobody in our family works so we go around robbing stuff all the time instead, and that the whole place is just full of alcos and druggies.'

'Maybe, yeah,' Kev said, but it didn't sound like he had really felt the same way. 'I dunno, I suppose I wasn't really thinking about it – I was trying to concentrate on getting picked.'

'How many of those lads from yesterday do you think have brothers who are addicted to heroin?' I said.

'None.'

'None, exactly. I can guarantee you. And then along comes the lad from Ballymun, who they already think they're better than, and he does.'

Nobody was near us in the park, except for a woman throwing a ball for her dog in the distance. It sounded like I was arguing with Kev, but he wasn't the one upsetting me.

'They think they're better than me too,' he said, 'and probably Taz and Jimmy too, even though they're not from Ballymun.'

'That's not the point, though. What if one of them found out about John?'

'So what if some fella at a Dublin trial finds out about your brother? What difference is that going to make?'

'Of course it makes a difference,' I said, and this time I *was* arguing with Kev. 'What happens if I get picked and then someone finds out? Do you think any of these other lads have ever seen a syringe in their lives except on the telly? Most of them have probably never even seen a lad smoking a spliff.'

We stopped walking but I kept talking.

'None of them are going to want to be on the same team as the lad whose brother is on heroin. Even if they didn't care, imagine what their parents would say? They'd probably have a heart attack. And what if Gerry Mangan or one of the coaches found out? They'd be watching me to make sure I'm not dealing in the corner of the dressing room.'

Kev laughed at that last part, which made me laugh a bit too, even though I was deadly serious.

'Have you talked to him at all since he came home?' Kev asked. 'Talked to him about it, I mean.'

'I don't want to talk to him,' I said. 'I don't have anything to say to him. He nicks everything in the house, disappears off for a few weeks and then comes back home laughing and joking like everything is normal.' Kev seemed surprised by how angry I was, but I kept going. 'And yeah, sure, he's back living at home, but we still don't know where he is most of the time. He just disappears off. I mean, I could go days at a time without seeing him, and the two of us share a bloody bedroom. Mam and Dad are in bits worrying about him, and there's nothing that any of us can do.'

I flicked the ball up into my hands and kicked it straight over the goalposts in front of us.

'He's not worried,' I said as we walked after the ball to get it. 'He doesn't care what anyone thinks about him or what they think about the rest of us. Otherwise he wouldn't be doing it.'

'So you changed your name?'

'Yeah.'

'I've some bad news for you so, buddy,' Kev said. 'He's always going to be your brother, no matter what. You could change your name to David Beckham and it wouldn't matter. You'd still be stuck with him, and you wouldn't be any better at taking free kicks. Or married to one of the Spice Girls.'

I knew he was trying to lighten the mood a bit and make me laugh, but it didn't work. 'You don't understand. I don't want to be the lad whose brother is addicted to heroin. I don't want our family to be that family. I don't want people looking at me and feeling sorry for me. Or looking at me and thinking they're better than me. I don't want anything to do with it.'

We kept walking up and down the same pitch until it started to rain, then we hid underneath a big tree to get a bit of shelter. Kev didn't ask about John again, and now that I'd figured out what was upsetting me so much by saying it out loud, I was happy to think about anything else. The rain ran down off the leaves over our heads, and I practised volleying the drops as they fell in front of me.

When it started to ease and looked like stopping, we walked back towards home, silently accepting that we couldn't stay out in the park forever and that, even if we could, Colm was unlikely to find us there.

Mam called me as soon as she heard the front door open. 'Philip, is that you?' she said frantically. 'Where have you been? Come here, quick.'

For a moment, I got this sinking feeling in my stomach. Had something happened to John?

Mam burst out of the sitting room before I could get

to her. 'Colm was here, you just missed him,' she said, and she was smiling like I hadn't seen her smile in a long time. In her hand, she was holding a small white envelope, clutching it tight. 'You got picked, Philip! You're in the academy!'

15

Mam and Dad and Kellie all gathered around me as I sat down on the couch to open the envelope. The Dublin GAA crest was printed in dark blue in the bottom right-hand corner. It really was from them. I unfolded the page carefully and started to read.

'Read it out loud there so we can all hear,' Dad said. The three of them crowded in beside me, trying to get a look over my shoulder. I read it slowly, making sure that I took in every word.

Dear Philly,

We are delighted to inform you that you have been selected to join the Dublin GAA football academy for the coming year.

The standard at this year's trials has been exceptionally high. Our warmest congratulations to you, your club and your family on your selection.

Along with this letter, you will have received a Dublin GAA kit bag, along with a Dublin GAA tracksuit, shorts and socks. Please wear this official team gear to your first academy training session on Sunday morning in Parnell Park, Donnycarney, at 10 a.m sharp, and to all future events at which you are representing Dublin GAA.

We're looking forward to seeing you again on Sunday, and to a successful season ahead.

Very best wishes – Áth Cliath abú!
Gerry Mangan
Head of Academy, Dublin GAA

When I finished reading it out loud, I went back to the start and read it again to myself. The words danced off the page: 'delighted to inform you'; 'exceptionally high'; 'representing Dublin GAA'.

I checked the name at the top again, just to be certain that it wasn't a mistake, but it wasn't. I had been picked for the Dublin academy. When I finally looked up from the sheet of paper in my hand, Mam and Dad and Kellie were all standing there staring at me.

'Look at all this gear Colm brought for you,' Dad said, falling over himself with excitement.

He picked up a kit bag, still in its plastic wrapper, and handed it to me. It smelled brand new. I turned it over in my hands and saw that it had the Dublin crest embroidered on the side.

'Colm said he knows a place that will do a lovely job stitching your initials into it, if you want, and on your tracksuit too,' Dad said, rubbing his hand over the crest to feel it. 'There's a guy out in Coolock who does it for all of the senior players.'

There was a tracksuit and knicks and socks and a few training tops, all stacked in a neat little pile on the floor, all in my size.

'I'm so proud of you,' Mam said, throwing her arms around me and squeezing me tight. 'So, so proud of you. You've worked so hard for this.'

'Yeah, well done, Golden Balls,' Kellie said, joining herself onto the hug; I hadn't heard that nickname for a while. 'Maybe I should give up the art and become a physio instead – what do you think?'

I held on to the both of them like I was holding on to the moment itself, trying to make it last forever.

I opened my eyes when I heard the sitting-room door squeak. I glanced over and saw John hanging back in the hallway, unsure whether or not he should come in.

'Well done, Philly. I knew you'd do it,' he said.

'Thanks,' I said, still smiling, and I turned back to Mam before my face started to drop. 'Did Kev get in?' I asked her, suddenly remembering.

'Oh, I don't know. Colm never mentioned.'

'And did you not ask him?' I said, ignoring the fact that I had only just thought to ask myself.

'No, sorry. I was so excited about your news that I completely forgot.'

I burst past John and out the front door and sprinted across the field and up the steps to Kev's flat. I knocked on the door and then realised that I was still holding my letter in my hand. I quickly folded it up and stuffed it into the pocket of my school trousers. I didn't want to be too excited in case Kev was disappointed.

When he opened the door, he was holding a navy tracksuit top in his hand with two sky-blue stripes running the length of the sleeves.

'You got in!' I said. Kev looked the way I felt.

'Yeah! Did you?'

'Yeah!' I said breathlessly.

'Are you serious?'

I pulled the letter back out of my pocket and waved

it like a lottery ticket. Kev ran out onto the balcony and jumped on top of me, and the two of us started shouting and cheering and celebrating, and if you didn't know any better, you'd swear we had just kicked the winning score in an All-Ireland final. Maybe some day but for now, right now, we were the kings of the world.

'We did it,' I said, clenching my fist with pure joy. I'd never seen Kev as happy in my life, but it felt as though I was looking at myself in a mirror.

'Yeow!' he roared, giving me a high five and a hug. 'Yup the flats!'

—

For a few days everything was fine again, until it wasn't.

Kev and I bounced into school the next morning as if we owned the place, practically begging someone to ask us if we had heard anything yet, just so we could tell them that we had got in. I even brought my tracksuit top with me in my schoolbag and the letter with the Dublin GAA crest on it, in case anyone thought we were making it up.

'Give us a look there,' Vinny Blake asked when I took out the tracksuit top so they could all see it. He reached over and tried to take it out of my hand.

'Get off,' I said, pushing him away with my arm. 'I only just got it last night. I haven't even tried it on yet.'

I had tried it on. It fit perfectly. I loved it already.

'The state of you,' Vinny said, doing his best to pretend that he hadn't really been that interested in the first place. 'You think you're great because you're after getting picked for some crappy little training squad. I bet you get dropped once they see you play for real.'

From behind us, there were a few hopeful *oooh*s at the thought of a scrap. I went to go for Vinny and give him a clatter, but Kev jumped between us and pushed me away just as Ms Breen walked into the room to start geography class.

'Shut up you, Vinny,' Kev sneered, walking me backwards towards my desk. 'How would you know? You weren't even good enough to get a trial anywhere.'

We left the Dublin gear at home when we went training that evening. Taz and Jimmy hadn't been picked. I felt bad for them, even though we all knew it was unlikely that the four of us would get picked and that at least one of us was going to end up disappointed. If it was me who had missed out and they had got in, I know I would have been gutted, so I decided not to mention the academy unless someone said it to me. Lots of them did, and Taz and Jimmy were the first two over to congratulate me and Kev. Colm made a short announcement before training to tell the rest of the team the news. I didn't know how to feel: I tried my best to look embarrassed at being singled out, but not so secretly, I was delighted.

We had no match that weekend, so Colm told me and Kev to take Thursday night off training to make sure we were well rested for our first session with the academy. Which is how I ended up on the couch at home, staying up late to watch a bit of *Forrest Gump* with Mam and Dad, when John tried to sneak in.

It was only because it was a quiet part of the film that we heard him. The click of the front door as the lock settled back into its latch was a giveaway, followed by slow, careful footsteps. Dad darted up from the couch and opened the door into the hallway. The light was off but there was nowhere in the shadows for John to hide.

He hadn't been home for days. I knew when he was missing because there was nowhere else for him to sleep other than in our room.

'Come here,' Dad barked. It caught me by surprise and made me jump. 'Where do you think you're going?'

John's hood was still pulled up. He was unsteady on his feet and his head was bobbing like he was listening to a song that only he could hear. 'To bed, I'm wrecked.' For such a short sentence, it took him a long time to say it; the end of each word went on for days. Mam picked up the remote from Dad's chair and put the TV on mute.

'Wrecked from what?' Dad said. His voice filled the room. 'Where have you been?'

He turned the light on in the hall. John squinted as if he'd just been sprayed in the face, but didn't answer.

Dad stared at John. 'Philly, go on to your room,' he said without turning around. I moved closer to Mam on the couch but made no attempt to get up and leave.

Dad's eyes never left John for a second. 'Right, come over here,' he said firmly. 'Now.'

John moved towards him slowly, putting his hand onto the wall for support, steadying himself, until the two of them were only a couple of feet apart. I had never seen him like this, and a pang of fear hit me. It wasn't a few cans of beer that had him this way.

'In here now, and empty your pockets onto the table,' Dad said.

'Leave me alone, would you. Who do you think you are, the guards?'

'You'll be wishing I was the guards if you don't do what I tell you right now.'

Hearing Dad speak to John like that, his orders cut with the toughness of his Belfast years, gave me a bit of a fright. He led and John followed. The TV turned to ads, flashing bright pictures of sandy beaches and crystal-clear blue swimming pools.

John emptied his right trouser pocket and then

his left – coins and keys and all sorts of rubbish, foil wrappers from chocolate bars and scrunched-up tissues. 'There. Are you happy now?'

Dad didn't react. 'Your jacket pockets too.'

John slowly turned one of his pockets inside out and made a big show of shaking out every last bit of fluff and dirt so Dad could see there was nothing in it.

'The other one, John,' Dad said. His voice didn't soften in the slightest; he sounded like he was losing patience, quickly.

'What's going on? Have you gone mental or something?' He looked at Mam, desperate for help. 'Ma, tell him to just let me go to bed.'

'Just do what you're told, John,' Mam said before Dad completely erupted, taking her hand from her face to speak.

I recognised the look on John's face. It was the same beaten look as the night when Mam had discovered her jewellery was missing, when he knew he had nowhere left to hide. As he turned out his other pocket, a little clear plastic bag, no bigger than a ten-cent bag of sweets from the shop, dropped onto the middle of the floor.

Dad's eyes widened. 'What's that?'

'It's nothing.'

'Pick it up off the floor and bring it over to me.'

John moved in slow motion, but he did as he was told.

Dad held the bag up to the light to inspect it. 'What's this?'

John looked panicked, as if he had just woken up and realised that his bad dream was real. 'It's nothing. It's not real or anything,' he said and tried to take it back out of Dad's hand.

'What do you mean?'

'It's only letting-on heroin, it just looks like it, it's not really heroin.'

I could feel Mam sink into the seat beside me at the mention of heroin and the sight of that little plastic bag that Dad had squeezed tightly inside his closed hand. I thought he was going to explode but he didn't.

'Oh, it's letting-on heroin?' he said calmly, pretending to be pleasantly surprised. 'Right, you come with me so.'

He grabbed John by the shoulder, spun him around and marched him back out the door and into the hall-way. I could hear them go into the bathroom.

'Wait, what are you doing?' John said. 'Amn't I after telling you that it's not real?'

'I don't care what it is. Not in this flat. Not a chance.'

'Wait, would you? Stop!'

But there was no more arguing, just the sound of the toilet flushing.

Dad came back into the sitting room alone, and a few seconds later, the bedroom door slammed.

On the TV, Forrest Gump was running.

16

Dad said he needed to go out for a walk to clear his head, which left me and Mam on the couch by ourselves. It was twenty to twelve, but Mam didn't want to go to bed either.

'Are you okay?' she said after a while, reaching over and resting her hand on top of mine.

I could hear John banging around in our room. I shook my head. 'I'm gonna sleep here tonight,' I said. 'I'm not sharing a room with him any more.'

I thought Mam would understand, but instead she

was annoyed. She pulled her hand away again. 'Stop, would you? Just go to bed and go asleep and don't be making things worse.'

I didn't mean to upset her. I tried to think of something to say, and when I looked back, tears were running down the side of her face.

'I don't know what to do. I just want him to get better,' she said, wiping her eyes with her fingers. 'I'm trying everything but nothing seems to be making any difference.'

I went into the kitchen and tore off a couple of sheets of kitchen roll and brought them back into Mam to use as a tissue.

'I found more of those little bits of tinfoil when I was cleaning last week.' She blew her nose into the paper and then scrunched it up into a ball. 'I asked him if he was back on it again, but he swore blind to me he wasn't, that they were from before. And I believed him.

'I shouldn't have listened to him,' she said, apologising as though she was to somehow to blame. 'That was stupid, wasn't it? But I wanted to. I just didn't think that he would keep lying to me.'

She started to cry again and I moved over beside her to give her a hug. I could feel her tears through my T-shirt.

'I rang a few people to see if they could help,' she said. 'Claire Mac gave me a number of a place that she knows in town. I went in and I met the man who runs it, and it looks okay. It's nothing fancy but it's clean.'

'What, like a rehab place?' I said. I had a picture in my head of a big room with white walls and hard plastic chairs set around in a circle, and John sitting there in a room full of strangers, telling them his story.

'Yeah, residential treatment they call it. I have a little leaflet that the man gave me,' she said, looking around for her handbag. 'I'll let you have a look later. Everyone has their own room, and they have to go to their meetings every morning, but then in the afternoon, they have other activities too.' Mam was almost excited to tell me about it, like she had finally found the answer she had been searching for.

'That sounds great,' I said enthusiastically. It felt like she was waiting to see how I'd react, and I wanted to be positive for her.

'I gave them all of our details so they could check and see if John qualifies,' she continued, 'and they rang me back the other day to say they have a place for him. But he has to be off it and completely clean before they'll take him.'

I agreed with Mam. This place sounded like it might really be able to help John. Hopefully it would be better than the Brickhouse. I thought back to the day when I went there with Kev, and that poor woman who couldn't escape from the drug dealer waiting for her outside. I didn't want John to end up like that.

'Have you talked to John about this?' I said, thinking of the little bag in Dad's hand and the desperation in John's voice as it went down the toilet.

Mam lowered her voice a bit. 'No, not yet. Sure, how could I? He hasn't been here in days, and then when he does come in …' There was no need to finish that thought. 'He knows I was looking for someone who could help him, but I haven't told him about this place yet. I'll talk to him in the morning, but I'm not asking him to go,' she said, already rehearsing that conversation. 'I'm telling him that he's going.' She looked over at the clock. 'I haven't slept in weeks,' she said. 'Much longer than that. Every night when you're all gone to bed, I lie there and I wait until I hear the door open and he comes in, but it doesn't open and then it's bright again.'

It was incredible how she kept going: getting up, going to work, coming home, making sure we were all okay. But when I looked at her closely now, I saw nothing but exhaustion.

'I know I can't be with him every second of the day, but it feels like that's what I need to do – do you know what I mean?'

'Yeah,' I said, but I also knew nobody else understood this problem in the same way that Mam did.

'Can you help me?' she said, reluctant to even ask.

'Of course,' I said. 'Anything.'

'When he's not here, I don't know where he goes or who he's with, but if you see him out on the blocks, stay close to him.'

I didn't fully understand what she was asking me to do.

'I know he brought that stuff home tonight, whatever it was, but he's obviously not thinking straight at the minute. If he knows that you're around, I don't think he'd do anything like that. He still loves you very much, you know.'

Mam's words caught me off-guard. John saying that he loved me was one thing, but they were only words unless he acted like it too, and that was all I cared about right now. Her plan made sense, though. He had always done his best to be a good example when I was around, a lot more than some of his friends did for their younger brothers, and no matter how deep in this hole he was, I couldn't imagine him using heroin if he knew I might catch him.

'I'm not asking you to start hanging around with him,' Mam explained. 'Go and play football with Kev or whatever you want to do, but if you can, be where you can see him and he can see you.

'Please, Philip,' she said. 'I need him to keep coming home at night. It's the only way I can be sure that he's okay. Please.'

—

At home, I was always trying to be where John wasn't. If he was lying sprawled on the couch in the sitting room, I would stay in our bedroom; when he came back into our room, I would quickly find a reason to leave. I made sure I was up before he woke in the mornings, and most nights I was either asleep, or pretending to be, when he came home. If he came home.

But once Mam asked me to watch him, when John went out, I went too. When I heard him leave the next evening, I waited until he had gone down the stairwell, then I counted to five in my head and slowly went after him. I didn't want him to know straight away that I was behind him, but I wanted to see where he was going.

He turned up the road and I followed him. He moved so slowly, dragging himself in the direction of the Towers, barely lifting his feet. From a distance, I could have mistaken him for an elderly man. Nineteen-year-old John had disintegrated into this frail shadow of skin and bone.

I hung back until he cut in off the road. The Friday-night buzz was in the air. Further up the road, I could see three lads my age on bikes, cycling in circles, waiting for somewhere to go, trying to outdo each other with skids and wheelies and bunny hops. I had a good look to see if I recognised any of them from school. I didn't want anyone I knew to see me with John.

He had stopped in front of one of the blocks and was talking to two men, his hands deep inside his pockets. Behind them, a mother held her young baby in one arm and her pram in the other, struggling to wrestle the two of them up the first flight of stairs towards her flat. I walked across the field, keeping an eye out for anybody that I knew; at least then I'd have a cover story when John asked.

I stopped when I got to the opposite end of the block that he was standing outside, and I started kicking my ball against the side of it. These walls taught me how to play football. For as long as I could remember, if there was nothing else to do – which was a lot of the time – I kicked my ball off the blocks. When I got it right, the ball bounced back off the concrete and came straight back into my hands like a boomerang, without me even needing to move. But if I got it wrong, it would end up on someone's landing or, worse, going through their window.

And sometimes, I got it wrong.

Tonight there was something relaxing, distracting, about the repetition. Right foot. Left foot. *Thump. Thump. Thump.* I didn't look over to see if John had spotted me yet, but I knew he would eventually.

'Yes, young fella, giz a pass,' someone shouted over to me as they walked by. He called me young fella, even though he was probably only two or three years older than me. If I passed it to him, there was no guarantee I'd get it back, but if I didn't, there was no guarantee he wouldn't just come and take it from me anyway.

I curled a lovely cross over to him, the lesser of two evils, and he controlled it on his chest with a perfect touch. His return pass was a little less accurate, though, sending me running in John's direction. I chased after the ball to get it back but John spotted me immediately.

'What are you doing up here?' he said, leaving the two men he was with and walking over to me.

'I'm just waiting for my friends,' I told him. 'We're going to have a match before it gets too dark.'

'Up here? What's wrong with down around our flats?'

'There's nothing wrong,' I said, not even acknowledging his suspicion. 'There's no one down there tonight. Kev and Al and Shane aren't around, so I said I'd come up here for a game with some of the lads from school.'

I turned the tables back on him. 'Anyway, what are you doing up here?' I asked.

John looked back over towards the two men he had come to meet, but they weren't paying us the slightest bit of attention. 'Nothing much,' he said. 'Just hanging around to see what the craic is.'

I flicked the ball back up into my hands and started bouncing it on the ground.

'Did Mam ask you to come up here?' John said as I turned to go back to where I had been kicking the ball off the wall. I stopped. 'Do you know what? It doesn't matter,' he said. 'I want to talk to you anyway. I feel like I haven't spoken to you in weeks. What's going on? How are you doing?'

He spoke quickly but there was genuine interest in his questions. He took his hands out of his pockets and started to fiddle with the zip on his jacket.

'Yeah, I'm grand,' I said, but stopped short of adding, 'Sure it's not like you care anyway.'

'Look, I'm sorry, I really am,' he said, trying to get me to have some sort of conversation. 'I'm sorry about last night. I'm sorry that you had to see all of that.'

'You think this is about last night?' I wanted to make him feel stupid for even attempting to apologise. 'You think that's what I'm annoyed over?'

He thought about what I'd said before answering. 'I know I'm after messing up, Philly. I do. But I'm trying to fix it.'

I wanted to ask how he thought he could fix anything, to ask him if he realised that the only fix was to never touch heroin or anything like it ever again, but I let him carry on.

'You think I'm only saying that. You think I don't care who I'm hurting, don't you? It's not true. I'm telling you it's not true.'

I thought of Mam lying awake in bed all night, unable to even distract herself to sleep, and I hoped John was thinking the same thing too.

'I've been chatting to this fella and he has a bit of work for me,' he told me. 'The money's not as good as the Meat Packers but it's grand. Better than the dole, like. I can start that in a couple of weeks, and I can start seeing if I can get my own place then, and soon I'll be out of your way and you won't have to worry about me any more.'

I hadn't spent more than five minutes with John since the night he was put out. He looked like a ghost, like all of the life and energy had been sucked out of his bones and all he had left was just about enough to get from one end of the day to the other. I couldn't see how anyone would give him a job.

'You don't believe me, do you?' he asked, and he sounded hurt, as though he'd lost me and his best would never be good enough any more.

'It sounds good,' I said, swallowing every other thought that I had for his sake, and he smiled at me.

'Me and the lads are just having a few cans and a smoke,' he reassured me. 'That's all, I promise. You don't need to be hanging around here anyway. There's loads of places you can play football.'

He held out his hand for a fist bump then took it back just as quickly when I left him hanging, stuffing it into his pocket. He went back to his friends and I stayed by myself, kicking the ball against the wall, until long after it got dark.

And when John finally decided it was time to go home, I waited for him to leave and then followed behind him.

17

Parnell Park appeared out of nowhere as we walked down the laneway, tucked away in its hiding place behind a neat row of houses. The posts of the floodlights, standing tall around the sides of the pitch, and the sloping roof of the stand were the only clues that would give it away. When we got to the big steel gates, they were open, waiting for us. A printed sheet stuck to one of them invited us in.

'Welcome to the Dublin GAA Academy,' I read aloud to Kev as the edges fluttered in the morning breeze.

'That's us,' he said proudly, and then pointed. 'Oh my God, look at that.'

The pitch was like a piece of artwork. It was the greenest grass I had ever seen, lit up in gold by the sun. It was cut to perfection, not a blade out of place, and marked out with fresh white lines just for us. Walking out onto it felt like walking into a photograph.

We were early but we weren't the first to arrive. A group had started to gather at the far end of the ground, and as we walked the length of the pitch to them, the atmosphere felt far more relaxed than on the day of the trials. Balls were whizzing through the air as lads chatted and introduced themselves to one another.

'I know you had to compete against each other to get this far,' Gerry Mangan said when everyone was there and we were ready to start. 'But you're not competing against each other any more. You're a team now, and you need to work as a team.'

He paused before he continued. 'I'm only going to say this to you because I've seen it happen before. When you walk through those gates, you're not a Kilmacud Crokes player or St Jude's player or a Plunkett's player – you're a Dublin player, and you're on Dublin time. So forget about club rivalries, and forget about Féile, and just concentrate on what you are here to do.'

I looked over to where Andrew Devanney was

standing, off to the side with the two other lads from St Christopher's. None of us knew who else had been picked until we arrived, but it was no surprise to see him there.

'Look, lads, it's really simple,' Gerry said. 'You're all here because you deserve to be here. You're here because we believe that you're the forty best players of your age in the county. That's already a huge achievement. You should be very proud of that.' He gestured towards the other coaches standing beside him. 'It's our job now to teach you, to coach you, to help you so you can keep learning and growing to be the best that you can be. Some of you will play senior football for Dublin one day and maybe even win an All-Ireland. Who is it going to be?'

I liked Gerry. He came across a bit serious but that was only because he was the man in charge. He reminded me a lot of Colm. When he spoke, he sounded like he really meant it. He didn't even know most of us yet, but I could already tell that he cared.

He introduced the other coaches, and one by one, they explained their plans for the year. There would be skills sessions and tactics sessions on the pitch. They would give us a workout programme of exercises that they expected us to do in our own time; they had even designed it so that we didn't need any weights or special equipment. 'Fifteen minutes every day,' that coach said. 'Just clear a bit of space in your bedroom and you're ready to go.'

They would teach us about good nutrition, about how to prevent injuries, about mental exercise and positive mindset. There was so much, it was hard to keep up, but the more I heard, the more excited I was.

For our first activity, they split us up into smaller groups. I made a point of introducing myself to everyone before we started, marching around, shaking hands – 'Howaya, I'm Philly' – which, it turned out, was the entire reason for the exercise. The rule was that you had to call a player by name before you passed them the ball. It was chaos. I was called Paulie and I was called Paddy and, at one point, I'm pretty sure I was called Willie. But by the time we were finished, we had a decent grasp of each other's names and a pain in our sides from laughing so much.

'They're great boots, aren't they?' I was having a drink of water between drills, and I recognised the lad who was walking over towards me. He was nearly a foot taller than me, with short black hair spiked up in a fringe at the front. He played in midfield for Kilmacud Crokes.

'I get a new pair every six months,' he said. He was wearing Predators too, though they looked like they had been through the wars compared to mine. 'How many of your lads got picked in the end?' he asked, looking around.

'Just two of us,' I said.

'Yeah, we were the same. Who else is here from your team – the quick lad who plays wing-forward?'

'Who, Taz? No, he didn't get picked.'

'Yeah, Taz,' he said, nodding. 'I remember that name now. He's a good footballer. I remember the first time we played you a few years ago, we thought you'd just try and kick us around the place, but you've some good players on that team. I'm David,' he said, and he held out his hand, still wearing his gloves.

'Ah, yeah, here we go,' I said sarcastically. 'Good old Ballymun, the lads from the flats, all they do is kick people.'

David turned bright red. 'No, no, I didn't mean it like that,' he started to splutter. 'It's just –'

I burst out laughing. 'Relax, relax, I'm only buzzing with you. That's nothing compared to what we normally have to put up with. Lads calling us every name under the sun because they don't like the sound of our accents. Their parents are worse too, most of the time.'

That was actually true – Kev had once been shouted at to go back to the flats by some woman on the sideline, all because he had won a 50/50 fair and square against her son. We were eleven at the time.

David's face was still on fire.

'I'm Philly, nice to meet you,' I said, remembering to finally shake his hand. The coaches were busy setting up the pitch for the next drill but they weren't ready for us yet. Andrew Devanney juggled a ball in the air from one foot to the other while we waited, doing keepie-uppies, and then, when he realised a few people were watching, he added a few tricks for good measure. I turned away and pretended to look for something in my bag. He loved the attention, but he wasn't going to get it from me.

His little performance was interrupted by one of the coaches who called us together to explain the next drill and then started reading names from his list, assigning us into different groups. I was on Team Four.

'One versus Two at the far end, Three versus Four in the middle, and Five versus Six here,' the coach announced as he sent us out around the pitch. As I jogged over to take my place, Andrew broke away from the rest of Team Three and came straight towards me to mark me. He smirked as he got closer but there was no hello and no handshake.

'I didn't expect to see you here,' he announced, hoping the others would turn to see who he was talking to. I ignored him and forced myself to remember what Gerry had told us at the start of the day: we were teammates now, I guess.

But when the drill started, it was clear that Andrew was playing by his own rules. He bustled and he barged, and he kept trying to catch me with his pointy elbows and make it seem like it was an accident. I ignored him the first time, and the second time too, but he kept at it, pure sneaky stuff, and it really started to get on my nerves.

'Get away from me, you little dope,' I warned him as I took another sly dig to the ribs. 'Try that again and I'll box the ears off you.'

I had no intention of hitting him, but he wasn't to know that. I knew the coaches were looking for good, clean defending, not fighting. When the next ball came in towards us, I read it perfectly and got to it first without touching him. He threw himself to the ground as if he'd been shot by a sniper, howling for a free kick.

'*Ref!*' he cried. 'Come on, sort it out. This is supposed to be football, not wrestling.'

'I'm watching, I'm watching,' the coach in charge said as he waved play on.

I turned around as Andrew picked himself up off the ground. 'Shut up crying, you rat, I never touched you.'

'Who do you think he's going to believe?' He smirked. 'Me or some little thief from the flats? Ballymunners rob your runners, isn't that right?'

I shaped as if I was going to swing for him, just to see him flinch. He jogged away, his hand in the air, calling for the ball again. I knew he was trying to get a reaction, to get me in trouble, but I wasn't going to bite and give him the satisfaction.

I decided the only thing I could do was fight fire with fire, so I played him the exact way I would if it was the last five minutes of a county final. Every time he took a step, I was right there with him. I pulled the sneaky stuff too, grabbing hold of his shirt for just long enough to disrupt his run, then letting go of it quickly before anyone spotted. I clipped his heels. I got enough of an arm or a leg on every ball to knock it away from him and stop him getting it cleanly. I didn't care about winning possession – I just wanted to be a nuisance.

And it worked. His team stopped passing in to him as often, worried that I would get there first, and he got more and more frustrated. As another ball bounced off his shins and rolled harmlessly out of play for a sideline ball, he spun around and got right into my face, squaring up to me. 'Get your hands off me,' he roared. He shoved me in the chest but I stood my ground. Everyone else might worship him but I wasn't going to be intimidated by him.

'Or what?' I smiled, winding him up. 'What are you going to do about it?'

He froze, unsure what to do, and then his face twisted into a look of pure nastiness. 'You're only a Ballymun junkie like the rest of them,' he said, spitting that horrible, ugly word at me.

I didn't decide to punch him. It just happened. I swung and I caught him, my fist slamming into his nose. He was so surprised that he didn't even make a sound. He dropped to his knees, his face in his hands, and stayed there. I waited for him to spring back to his feet, to lunge at me and try to hit me back, but he didn't. There wasn't going to be a fight; it was already over. One punch. One lash of rage, a pure reflex. That was it.

He pulled his hand away from face, studying it for blood. There was none. 'Go on back to the flats,' he said. He was holding back tears, but his voice was still dripping with superiority. Before I could go for him again and make him really sorry, the coach raced over to see what had happened.

'All right, all right, all right.' He put himself in between the two of us and looked at Andrew, who was still making a show out of holding his face. 'What's going on?'

Before I could even try to explain my way out of trouble, one of the other St Christopher's players butted in. 'He punched him in the face,' he said, pointing his finger at me. 'I saw it all.'

'Is this true?' the coach asked Andrew.

He took his hand away from his face and then slowly

started to touch his nose with the tips of his fingers, wincing every time. 'Yeah, I think my nose might be broken,' he said, milking it.

The coach turned to me. A little vein popped out of the side of his head, just below where his hairline started, but he didn't shout. 'Did you punch him?' he said calmly.

'Yeah, but –' I started to tell him that there was another side to the story, that I had been provoked, but I was cut off after two words.

'I don't want to hear it. You' – he turned back to Andrew – 'go and get checked and make sure there's nothing broken. There's an ice pack in the first aid kit if you need it. And you,' he said, summoning me with the curly finger, 'come with me. Now.'

He marched me over to where Gerry Mangan was standing, steering me with a firm hand on my back, and I waited while the two of them spoke privately and decided what should happen next.

'Do you want to tell me your version?' Gerry asked me as the coach left and walked back to our group. 'And be quick about it, please.' He sighed. 'I really don't have time for this sort of messing.'

I told him exactly what had happened: how there had been a little bit of pulling and dragging, but that we'd both been as bad as the other in that respect. 'Then he started having a go at Ballymun and the flats. He called me a thief and said that I go around robbing runners,' I explained, getting more agitated.

Gerry's face didn't change. He didn't seem to think there was anything wrong with what Andrew had said.

'And then he called me a junkie,' I blurted. I could barely get the word out. I didn't even want to repeat it – it was horrible. 'He said that everyone in Ballymun is a junkie. So yeah,' I admitted, 'I gave him a smack so he'd shut up. But I only hit him once, and he deserved it for saying stuff like that.'

Gerry didn't interrupt me and waited until he was sure I had finished everything that I wanted to say. 'Okay, thank you. I didn't realise that was what had happened.' He thought for a moment. 'I have no time for any of that stupid slagging,' he said sympathetically. 'We've players here from all over Dublin, and we expect everyone to show a little maturity and get along with one another.'

I hoped that would be the end of it, that Gerry would see both sides and send me off to shake hands with Andrew and apologise. We would all move on and get back to training.

'But discipline on the pitch is every bit as important as anything you can do with a football,' he continued. 'I have a responsibility to look after everyone while they're here, and I can't have players throwing punches at other players. It's unacceptable. I'm sorry, I have to send you home.'

'No, please.' I panicked as everything unravelled. I couldn't be sent home early on the first day for fighting. 'You can't do that – it's not fair. You can't send me home for the rest of the day. I'm sorry. I promise it won't happen again.'

Gerry shook his head, as if I hadn't understood what he had just told me. 'No, it's not just for the rest of the day. I'm very sorry, I have no choice. I have to withdraw your place in the academy.'

18

walked back to Ballymun by myself, but I didn't go home. I could have explained to Gerry that I needed to wait for Kev, that Trish was supposed to pick the two of us up together, but I didn't see what good that would do me; he had asked me to leave. I didn't even tell Kev what had happened or that I was going. He was in the middle of a drill, and I wanted to get out of there as quickly as possible. He would figure it out for himself.

When I got near Ballymun, I kept going and headed towards Colm's house instead. I couldn't think of anywhere else to go. There was no point going home and telling Mam and Dad; they wouldn't know what to do. But Colm would. I climbed over the wall, taking extra care not to catch my Dublin tracksuit on any sharp edges. The way things were looking for me, I might never get another one again.

Colm was in his front garden, wrapping the cable around the handle of his lawnmower while he chatted to his next-door neighbour, an older man who was just about to head out. The smell of freshly cut grass met me before I even got to the gate. Colm was surprised to see me.

'Can I talk to you?' I said. 'I have something I need to tell you. It's important.' And then I added, 'I think I'm in trouble.'

His neighbour made a quick excuse to leave and told Colm he'd chat to him later. I told Colm the entire story, from start to finish, before he even had a chance to ask me if I was all right or if I wanted to come inside.

Colm let me finish everything that I wanted to say before he spoke. 'I know,' he said.

'What do you mean?'

'I know about what happened already.' He tapped his pocket. 'Gerry Mangan phoned me a few minutes ago.'

Hope flickered for a second. 'What did he say?' I asked, looking for the smallest thing to cling on to. 'Are they really going to kick me out of the academy over this?'

But Colm didn't answer that question. 'I appreciate you coming straight here to tell me yourself,' he said. 'You could have gone home and waited for me to find out some other way, or waited to tell me at training on Tuesday when lots of other people were around. It takes courage to own up to your mistakes like that, so thank you.'

It was nice to feel like I had done something right for a change. 'I need you to help me,' I said.

Colm looked puzzled. 'Have I not been helping you since the first day I met you?' He said it softly, and if he was angry with me, he was careful to make sure it didn't sound like it. 'I helped you by picking you for the trials in the first place. I helped you by ringing Gerry and convincing him to let you go down even though you were injured. I'm always helping you,' he said, and that puzzled look made a bit more sense now. 'When are you going to start helping yourself? That's what I want to know.'

Colm was right and I didn't know what to say. I'd have preferred if he was angry; seeing him disappointed was so much worse. 'I'm sorry,' I said. 'What am I going to do?'

'What do you want me to say? You want me to tell you that it will all be grand, that I can fix this for you, is that it? Because I don't think I can.'

A wave of worry washed over me, and all I wanted to do was turn and run. To keep running and never look back.

'I really thought this was going to be the first step towards something special for you,' he said. 'Do you realise the opportunity you've just lost?'

And for the first time, I did truly realise. Even when Gerry Mangan was sending me home, deep down inside I had convinced myself it would somehow all be okay, like when the teacher puts you out of the class then calls you back inside a few minutes later with a final warning to behave. They didn't want to kick me out of the academy, I told myself; they just wanted to teach me a lesson and give me a fright.

Now I wasn't so sure.

'Why did you let it get to you?' Colm asked. 'Why do you care what someone like Andrew Devanney thinks? He doesn't know anything about Ballymun. He doesn't have a clue about the community that's here and how much its people care about each other. The only thing he sees is a stereotype, that Ballymun is a bad place where bad things happen. But I know that's not what Ballymun is about, and you know that's not what Ballymun is about. Just because someone ignorant thinks it doesn't make it true.'

'That's why I hit him,' I protested, glad that someone could finally see where I was coming from. 'I was defending Ballymun. I wasn't going to let him stand there and mouth off with that rubbish and not do anything about it.'

That was true, but all my life, people had talked down Ballymun and looked at us like we were pieces of dirt because of where we lived, and I had trained myself to ignore it. It wasn't easy. It still hurt every time, but I never wanted to let those people see that hurt. I never wanted to give them the satisfaction.

But when Andrew used the word 'junkie', it touched a nerve. I couldn't explain that to Colm, though. I still hadn't told him about what was going on with John.

'Did it work?' Colm asked me.

'Did what work?'

'You thought you were standing up for Ballymun by hitting him, but all you did was prove him right.'

His words hit me like a sledgehammer. Colm was right. I could picture Andrew going around telling everyone about the little thug who had started on him at the trials and got expelled from the academy for it – 'Typical Ballymun, what do you expect?' I suddenly started to feel a bit dizzy.

Colm wound another few loops of the lawnmower cord around the handle while he let the truth sink in with me.

'What do I do now?' I asked. 'Will they let me back in?'

He shook his head. 'I don't know, to be honest. I'll speak to Gerry again tomorrow or the next day when everything has calmed down a bit, but I don't think so.'

He started gathering up little clumps of cut grass from the ground to put them into the bin. I waited for him to continue, but he just kept collecting the grass, not saying a word.

'I'm sorry,' I said again, and I meant it, but this wasn't a situation I could apologise my way out of. Maybe it had been a mistake to come and see Colm. I'd thought he might be able to help me fix things, but I hadn't realised how hurt he would be.

'You do realise that this wasn't just about you?' he said. 'You were in that academy as a Ballymun Kickhams player. You were there representing the team, the club, me. Your family. Everyone from Ballymun.'

I felt tiny. I could feel the tears starting to build but I blinked them away. I wouldn't cry here, not in front of Colm.

'I'll call Gerry, and I'll see you at training on Tuesday evening.' Colm stepped onto the path outside his house, a sign that this conversation was over for now and it was time for me to leave. 'Whatever happens, though, I think, for the moment, it would be better if someone else captained the team.'

He took his time with each part of the sentence, choosing his words carefully. It was like a quick slap in the face or being blindsided by a sucker punch – there was no reaction at first, only numb shock, while the rest of my body took a moment to catch up with my brain and realise what was happening. I couldn't believe what he was saying. I was suddenly aware that I was getting very warm, like that flash of fever in the seconds before you throw up.

'What? No.' I swallowed. 'Colm, it was a mistake. One second, I forgot myself for one second, that's all.' Now I really was getting upset. 'All I want is to play for Dublin and you're telling me I've ruined that. Is that not enough of a punishment? You don't have to take the captaincy off me as well.'

But Colm had made his mind up. 'It's someone else's turn,' he said, and I knew that even if I did let myself cry, my tears wouldn't help to change his mind.

'For how long?' I asked.

'I don't know. I'm not sure. Prove to me that it was just a mistake, that it won't happen again. Prove to me that you've learned from it. We'll see then.'

He turned to go back and finish his work in the garden. 'I'll see you on Tuesday,' he said.

He wouldn't see me on Tuesday, though. He wouldn't see me at training for a long time.

—

I was still stunned, in an angry daze wandering in the vague direction of home, when Shane jammed on the brakes of his bike and skidded in front of me. He came out of nowhere, his back wheel scraping the ground as he whipped the bike around to stop perfectly, about a foot away from me. I jumped a little with the fright, and Shane burst out laughing. Mission accomplished.

Al cycled over behind him. 'Well, what's the story? What are you up to?' He spotted the tracksuit and the bag. 'Did you have your Dublin thing today?'

'Yeah,' I said, silently hoping there wouldn't be too many more questions.

'How'd it go?' Al said. There was no point in lying. They would hear the full story from Kev in school tomorrow anyway.

'Bad,' I said and I laughed, a bit of bravado to cover up how I really felt. 'I got sent home for punching some lad.'

Al and Shane reacted as if it was the funniest thing they had ever heard. 'Ye bleedin' thick, what did you do that for?' Shane said.

'I dunno, he was annoying me so I gave him a slap.' And then for good measure, I added, 'He said I was after breaking his nose,' as if that somehow made it all worthwhile.

Al nodded in appreciation. 'Where are you going now then?'

'Home.'

'Stall it with us. We're going around to the pub to play pool, and the United match is on TV as well.' Al checked his watch, and I realised that I hadn't a clue what time it was. 'Come on,' he said to both me and Shane. 'The match is starting in a few minutes. It'll be easier for us to get on the pool table while everyone is watching that. Let's go.'

The pub was around the corner on the main road, wedged in between our run-down shopping centre, which had more closed shops than open ones, and the garda station. I had only been inside a couple of times. The lads liked it because the barmen didn't mind if they came in to play pool at the weekends, and then, depending on who was working and who else was in there, they would try to sneak a drink as well sometimes.

I didn't mind playing a few games of pool and watching whatever match was on, but I was never that interested in drinking. You couldn't drink and play football – at least not the way I wanted to play – and I knew which one I was choosing. I had tried a sip out of a warm can of cider that Al and Shane were sharing in the field one night when we were a little younger, and it was rank. I spat it straight back out.

The two lads chained their bikes to the fence at the side of the pub and the three of us went inside and up the stairs. Shane opened the door and a rush of heat hit us. It was a lovely day but inside it was dark. The blinds were all pulled down, but as the light from outside followed us in through the door, I could see the pub was packed with people sitting in twos and threes and fours on small stools around little circular tables, every eye in the place on the football. A big screen took up the whole of one wall, with a projector hanging overhead, and spread out high in the corners were a few other smaller TVs. United and Chelsea had just kicked off, and it was still 0-0. They barely even noticed us as we came in.

We snaked our way through the tables down to the back where the pool table was. Two men were finishing up a game, down to the last two balls on the table, one stripe and the black ball. Al took a two-euro coin out of his pocket and put it down on the corner of the table to let them know we were playing next.

I had played enough pool to know the rules, but I wasn't very good. John had tried to teach me. I'm not sure if he was naturally good at it or if he just played a lot and got good at it that way, but pool was his thing. Him and Aaron had even been picked to go away with an Irish youth team once or twice while they were still in school. John showed me all these different techniques – how to get the right spin on the ball, the different angles to use – but I was never that interested in learning from him. I just wanted to rack the balls up, lift off the plastic triangle and smash them as hard as I could.

I pushed the thought of John out of my head. I didn't want to think about him. This whole mess that I was in was his fault anyway. If he wasn't on heroin, I never would have snapped when Andrew used the word 'junkie'. I'd heard people use the word 'junkie' all the time – lads on the blocks, lads in school, I'd even used it myself, I'm sure – but it felt different now. I realised how horrible it was. It felt personal.

Al moved the corner of one of the blinds and looked out the window while we were waiting for our turn to play. He motioned for us to follow him as he pushed open the fire exit and went out onto the balcony that ran along the back of the pub. A small steel bin stood outside, topped with cigarette butts and ashes, and Al nudged it over with his foot so it held the door open for us and we wouldn't get locked out there. He leaned on the steel railing, looked down over the side and waited for us to come and do the same. 'This is what I was telling you about,' he said to Shane, and then he turned to me. 'What do you think of those?'

The pub's balcony overlooked the back yard of the garda station next door, where a half-dozen motorbikes were lined up in two rows, all different shapes, sizes and colours. They looked amazing.

'That blue one down the end is class,' I said, pointing

to the one that had really caught my eye. There was a huge cheer, and when I looked back inside, I could see the red jerseys celebrating on the TV. United were already 1-0 up.

'Mark was telling me about these,' Al said. 'They're all nicked.' Mark was Al's uncle but he was only a little bit older than us. I think he was 16, but he might have been 17.

'How do you know?' I asked.

'They're from a raid,' Al explained. 'When they're reported as stolen and the guards find them, they store them out the back here for a few weeks before they bring them back to the owners.' He lowered his voice. 'But Mark was saying that because they were all nicked in the first place, the steering lock is already broken on them most of the time, and they've already been hotwired too.' We were the only ones out on the balcony, but Al was doing his best to hide his excitement. 'So, if you wanted to, you could just hop the wall into the yard, open the gate' – he touched the tips of his two forefingers together and made a noise like an electrical buzz – 'and then, bingo bango, you drive off on your new motorbike.'

He looked thrilled with this discovery. It wasn't unusual for a group of lads to show up at the flats with a stolen motorbike, and any time they did, it instantly became the centre of attention. Everyone else was drawn to it like a magnet, an audience gathering around while the lads with the bike zipped around the field, the rubber of the tyres tearing chunks out of the soft grass and leaving a zig-zag of deep tracks. The rest of us could only watch on jealously. In my head, I imagined what it would be like to take that lovely blue motorbike for a quick spin around the field.

Al finally got to the point, and I realised that maybe he hadn't really brought us up here to play pool. 'Mark was saying we should come with them the next time,' he said, looking back over his shoulder to make sure that nobody had come outside for a smoke. 'That gate isn't even properly locked most of the time, apparently. It's just a bar you can slide across.' He glanced over to Shane to see what he thought. 'We can do the gate or something while the lads get the bikes. It's easy.'

I had seen Al and Shane rob bikes before – bicycles, though, not motorbikes. One time when I was with them, Shane walked up to this lovely mountain bike that was propped up unlocked against the front window of a shop and wheeled it away. Loads of people were coming in and out of the shop and passing by who could have grabbed him and stopped him, but nobody did. If he had got a bit of a chase from someone, it would have been all the better. Al and Shane were bored, and this was just a game to them.

What Al was suggesting now was serious business, though. I didn't have any interest in robbing motorbikes, and even if I did, I'd think of somewhere better to rob them from than a garda station. Talk about asking for trouble. Something told me this plan wasn't quite as straightforward as Mark had made it sound.

'What happens if you get caught?' I asked, curious to know if Al had even considered that possibility.

It was a fair question but he looked at me like I was a dope. 'They've done it two or three times now and they've never been caught. They do it when the guards are out on patrol in the car. One person keeps sketch from up here, and someone else stands out the front and does the same, and everyone else gets the bikes out before the guards come back.'

'Anyway,' he continued, 'even if one of us got caught, we'd be grand. If it's your first time, they're only allowed to give you a JLO.'

A JLO was a Juvenile Liaison Officer, a special guard that came to your house to meet you and your parents if you got arrested. Ronnie Conway from school had a JLO, but he ended up in court eventually because he kept on robbing things. The judge fined him and said he'd give the money to the poor people, which didn't make sense. Ronnie Conway's family didn't have much themselves; the judge could have just let them keep the money.

'I'm in anyway,' Shane said. I didn't answer; a knock on the door from a JLO was the last thing Mam and

Dad needed.

'Nice one,' Al said. 'We'll probably make a few quid too. They usually keep the bike for a day or two to rally around and have a bit of a laugh, and then they sell it on to some other lads who want to have a go.' He rubbed one hand off the other as if he was counting out banknotes. 'Buy low, sell high: isn't that what they said in business studies?'

I was amazed that he had been paying attention to anything at all that was said in school.

'Supply and demand,' Shane agreed as a door opened below us. The three of us ducked back inside the pub and watched as a guard pushed a bike out into the yard. He couldn't have heard us talking but we still didn't want him to spot us, even though there was no law against standing on the balcony – actually, maybe there was, seeing as we shouldn't even have been in the pub in the first place.

Inside, the pool table was empty. Al passed Shane a cue and started to rack the balls. 'Why are you always such a little chicken?' he said, mocking me because I still hadn't given him an answer. 'Don't come if you don't want to.'

I didn't want to. But a couple of weeks later when they were going, I had nothing better to be doing, so I went with them anyway.

19

t was time.

It had been five minutes since the garda car disappeared off the main road, and there had been no sign of it since. The sun had slipped away at just the right moment for us – this wasn't something you'd try in broad daylight – and the darkness was our friend. Even as the bright yellow lamps of the streetlights flickered into action, there were plenty of pockets where we could hide.

Mark was standing in the shadows across the road with one of his friends, and Shane was with them too.

Another friend had gone upstairs to the balcony of the pub so they could keep an eye on things in the station yard. I pressed my hands into the side of the bus shelter and stared up the road. I concentrated on the crossroads where the squad car had turned in towards the Towers, afraid to look away in case I missed something, while Al ran through the instructions with me one last time.

'What are you worrying about?' he said. 'All you have to do is stand there, and if you see them coming back, give us a whistle. It's easy.'

Easy? Learning how to ride a bike was easy. Learning how to help steal one from a garda station – a motorbike, at that – was not.

Al could tell that I was uneasy, and I knew the feeling was mutual. They needed someone to keep sketch out the front, and he had convinced Mark that I would be able to do it, but he didn't trust me not to chicken out. It was like he could read my mind. As I looked out into the darkness, the only thing I could think of was what would happen to us if we were caught.

Al and Shane were used to this. They were nervous too, but that was where they got the buzz. That was the whole reason for doing it in the first place. Out of all of my friends, they were the two who were always involved in some sort of messing – Al more than Shane, to be honest, but wherever you found one, you found the other. They had gas stories, telling us about the trouble they had gotten into or, even better, the near misses and the chases. The stories were fun, but from a safe distance. I never wanted to be in the thick of it myself. And they never really asked me to go with them.

Besides, I always had an excuse, whether it was training or a match or just having a kickabout with Kev and the others. Or, at least, that used to be the case. It was a Tuesday night. I should have been at training but I had stopped going after the fight in the academy, and I hadn't been back since. What was the point? I had done everything I was supposed to do, I had put all of that time and effort into trying to be the best I could be, and then as soon as I made one mistake, it was all taken away from me. What annoyed me most was the feeling that everyone expected me to mess up, everyone expected me to cause trouble because of where I came from, and as soon as I did, they slammed the door shut on me again.

Kev couldn't understand why I had stopped going to training. When we were in school, he kept asking me if I was coming with him that evening, and even if I said no or lied and said that I wasn't feeling well, he'd still knock up to the flat for me as usual when he was going. Colm had made him captain instead of me, but Féile would be starting in a few weeks' time and Kev really wanted me to come back. Now that school was finished, and we were on our summer holidays, it was a bit easier to avoid the constant questions and, eventually, he got the message and stopped asking.

I started to hang around more with Al and Shane. They liked being with Mark and his friends because a few of them were 18, so there was always plenty of smokes and cans to go around. We'd sit there all night and they'd pass it all around, and none of them could understand why I didn't even want to try, how I wasn't even a little bit curious. John had always told me he'd bash me if he caught me drinking, and told his friends he'd bash them if he saw them giving me any. Part of me thought he should have taken his own advice. The other part thought that maybe he wished he had: that's why it was worth listening to. I decided to trust him.

I started to bring a little can of Lynx deodorant in the pocket of my jacket, and when I left the lads to go home, I sprayed myself from head to toe. I didn't want Mam and Dad to smell the smoke on my clothes. Kellie copped me out in the field one night, a few blocks down from where we normally hung out. She was walking by with a few of her friends when she saw me and told me to go home. I could see that she was having a good look, and when she saw that I didn't have a can or a cigarette in my hand, she didn't seem too fussed and headed off.

Every night without fail, one of the lads mentioned the motorbikes in the garda station, and after that, it was all we talked about. We talked about it so much that eventually it turned into a plan, and once it was a plan, nobody could back out. Which is how I ended up here, standing by myself in a battered old bus shelter that had seen better days, watching anxiously for a squad car that I hoped would never arrive.

Al scampered across the road to join the others before I could change my mind and back out. I quickly counted the four of them before I lost them again in the darkness. The black tracksuits and black jackets blended into the night, and all I could make out was the white of their runners, scrambling up and over the wall, and they were gone.

We all knew the plan inside out. They only needed two or three minutes, enough time for Mark and Tom, his friend, to get two bikes started while Al and Shane opened the gate. From the balcony of the pub, we couldn't tell if the gate was locked properly, but Mark had brought a bullsnips and given it to Shane in case they needed it to snap the lock in a hurry. Once they had the gate open and the bikes started, Al and Shane would jump on the back with the two lads and the four of them would get out of there before they got caught. I'd meet them all again later back up on the blocks.

The headlights of a car lit up the bus shelter and I put my fingers to my lips, ready to sound the alarm as I squinted straight down the beams. It came towards me slowly, as if the driver was looking for something or someone. He looked out the window at me as he passed, and I caught his eye, but he drove on by; probably out delivering a takeaway and trying to find his turn. I put my hands back in my pockets. I'd never hear the end of it if I panicked and whistled them all back for no good reason.

I tried to imagine that I was sitting up on top of the wall, looking down into the yard and watching the lads as they ducked and dived in the shadows. The wall was about twelve-foot high; Shane and Al had gone first, getting a boost from the two older lads, and then they had helped to pull them up on top of the wall. Surely they had been gone for two minutes. I thought I'd at least hear the motorbike engines as they started up. What was taking them so long?

There was a big drop on the far side of the wall. Maybe one of them had rolled their ankle when they jumped down and now they were stuck, hiding at the bottom of the wall, trying to figure out how to get back out. Maybe Mark had got it all wrong and the bikes weren't hotwired or the steering locks were still on. Maybe Shane couldn't get the bullsnips to cut the lock.

The slam of a car door snapped me out of it, and so did the sight of the guards crossing the road and heading straight for the front door of the station. My heart jumped right up into my mouth. I'd been expecting them to drive past me and pull up in the empty spaces right in front of the station if they came back, but they'd come from the other direction and parked away from the station for some reason, and I had never even heard them pull in. I whistled as loud as I could. I needed to be sure that the lads would hear me.

The sound split the night, and before I was even done, the guards stopped dead and spun around to stare straight at me. I had to clench my fists just to stop my hands from shaking. There were two of them, a man and a woman. The male guard said something to his partner, too quietly for me to hear, and then he walked towards me while she carried on inside. He reached his hand inside his jacket pocket as he crossed back over the road and pulled out a black notebook and a stubby little pencil.

'What are you up to?' he said. When he spoke, he had a country accent. All of the guards in Dublin were from the country. I don't think I'd ever met a Dublin guard. Where did all the Dublin guards go, I wanted to ask, but being smart now wasn't going to do me much good.

'Me? I'm just waiting for the bus,' I said, looking around as if I wasn't sure who he was speaking to.

'The bus, yeah? And who else is with you?' he said.

'No one.'

'Who are you whistling at then?' he said, his eyes narrowing a little as he took a few more steps towards me. He was tall and looked strong, and he was close enough now that he could have reached out and grabbed me by the collar of my jacket if he wanted to. He couldn't do that, though. I hadn't done anything wrong, and if he touched me, Mam and Dad could go down to the station and report him.

'I just like whistling,' I said, deciding it was better to play dumb rather than get too cheeky. 'I was going to do a song.' I was hoping he'd decide there were more serious crimes than hanging around bus stops and whistling and just send me home. I looked straight past him to see if I could spot the lads trying to climb back over the station wall, but there was still nothing.

He noticed me watching the wall, and he turned to see what I was looking at. 'Stay there,' he told me, and he walked in a circle around the shelter and reappeared on the other side.

I knew what was coming next: name and address, please, and then he'd write it into his notebook and tell me to go home. That was always the way with the guards, even though I was never really in trouble. Any time they saw two or three of us hanging around, they thought we must be up to something and told us to move on. 'Loitering' was one of their favourite reasons, or 'anti-social behaviour'. There must have been boxes full of notebooks inside in the station with pages of our names and addresses, and plenty of fake ones too. What was the point?

Except, this time, he didn't ask me for any of those details. 'Go on away home and don't be messing,' he said.

'What messing? I didn't do anything,' I said. The guard folded his arms across his chest, and I didn't need to be told twice. 'All right, I'm going, I'm going.'

He stood and watched me as I started walking up the road. I hadn't gone more than a couple of steps when I heard the lads hurrying back over the wall.

'Go go go, leg it,' Al shouted. The entire garda station lit up in an instant, front and back, as bright as a football stadium with floodlights hitting every inch of it. Two guards burst through the front door just in time to see the four lads land like cats and hit the ground running as they tore off down the road.

They went in four different directions, forcing the guards to split up. I didn't need to be told what to do. I already had a bit of a head start on the guard who had been speaking to me.

'Hey! You! Get back here now,' he roared as he started to chase me. 'You're under arrest.'

His footsteps were heavy on the ground, and with every stride, they sounded like they were getting closer. He could move for a big man. Still, I was faster, and Ballymun might have been his beat, but it was my home. I could get lost in a second. Up ahead, a car was stopped at the traffic lights, and as the lights turned green and it pulled away, I saw my opportunity. I darted in behind it, sprinting across the road. The guard had to break stride to avoid getting knocked down, and by the time he'd crossed, it was too late. I was gone.

I wasn't running towards our flat any more, I realised. I was running away from it, but that was better than leading him right up the stairwell and to the front door. Mam didn't need to know about this, and Dad especially didn't. I knew the guard wouldn't give up the chase easily, but when I finally stopped, I couldn't hear his footsteps any more. All the lights were off in the house that I'd stopped outside. I went into their garden and crouched down behind the front hedge to listen. I waited for a minute or two, long enough to be sure that the coast was clear. I was safe.

I was sweating and still out of breath when I pushed the door of our flat open a few minutes later. 'It's me, I'm home,' I called to Mam and Dad. I didn't go in to say hi and went straight to my bedroom instead. If they asked, I'd tell them we'd been playing football. I sat down on the edge of the bed with my heart hammering in my chest so loud that I could hear it in my ears. Where were the others?

The knock on the front door made me jump. I froze where I was, as if whoever was standing outside might hear me if I moved as much as an inch.

'Get that there, please, Philip, will you?' Mam called from the couch. 'Did you not tell your friends you were coming in for the night?'

It might have been Al or Shane, breathless as well, coming to check that I'd got away too and to tell me about their chase and how they'd managed to escape. But I had a bad feeling. It didn't sound like the lads' knock, a friendly knock. It was a man's knock, an angry knock, looking for someone.

How had the guard figured out where I lived? He couldn't have followed me. I'd definitely lost him before I came home. Maybe another guard had caught one of the lads and they were in the station now, and they'd had to tell them who was with them and where I lived.

Bam-bam-bam.

'Philip, are you getting that?' Mam asked again. 'Don't have me getting up, please.'

'Yeah, I have it.'

It was better to get it myself anyway. At least then I could try to talk my way out of trouble before Mam and Dad realised that it was a guard at the door.

I took a deep breath and got my story straight, but when I opened the door, it wasn't who I was expecting.

20

'Do you mind if I come in for a minute?' Colm asked. I hadn't seen him since the afternoon when we'd spoken in his front garden. 'I'm glad to see you're still out keeping fit anyway.'

I ran my hand over my face to wipe the sweat away. My heart had just about stopped thumping after sprinting home, but it started again just as quickly when I saw Colm standing there. I hadn't told Mam and Dad that I had been expelled from the academy, and they didn't know that I hadn't been training either. I had been out with Al and Shane in the evenings, and most Saturdays too, so they hadn't suspected anything.

'Who's at the door, Philip?' Mam popped her head out from the sitting room before I could find out why he had called or think up a good cover story. 'Colm,' she said, delighted. 'Come on in, Phil's inside here. You'll have a cup of tea, will you? The kettle's on.'

I followed the two of them back inside. Mam went into the kitchen to get the cups from the press, giving them a quick rub with a tea-towel while she waited for the kettle to finish boiling, and I showed Colm into the sitting room. Dad got up to shake his hand and gestured for him to make himself comfortable on the couch.

'Well now, how's everything going with the football?' Dad asked as he sat back down. I was still standing over by the hall door, unsure what this was all about.

'It's actually just your parents that I wanted to speak to,' Colm said to me, 'if you wouldn't mind giving us a minute, please.'

I had no idea why Colm had called, but if Dad spotted the look of confusion on my face, he completely ignored it. 'Of course,' he said, turning to me and nodding towards my room. 'Close over the door there behind you, please, good lad.'

I did as I was told, but I left the sitting-room door open slightly and did the same with my bedroom door, hoping I might be able to catch part of the conversation without making it obvious. They spoke for about ten minutes before Dad called me back inside.

'Have you anything you want to tell us?' Dad asked while Mam topped up their cups with another drop of tea. I had lots of things that I *should* tell them but nothing that I particularly *wanted* to, but if I didn't explain what was going on now, Colm surely would, so I went through the whole story from the beginning.

When I had finished, Mam said, 'We know.'

'How?' Colm had told them already, I presumed.

'Well, for one thing, you haven't taken your boots out of your bag in weeks.'

'Oh.'

'Why didn't you tell us what was going on?' She sounded disappointed.

'It's grand. I didn't want you to be worrying about me. The two of you have enough to be worrying about.'

I forgot for a moment that Colm was sitting there too, and I was afraid that I had said too much.

'It's okay,' Mam said, reading my mind. 'We explained everything to Colm.'

I glared at Mam. If I'd wanted Colm to know about our family business, I would have told him myself. 'Just now?' I asked.

Colm turned his chair slightly to face me. 'No, I

called over last week to see if you were okay and find out if you had fallen off the face of the earth,' he said. 'You were out, but I had a good chat with your mam and dad instead. I'm very sorry to hear about John. You must be so worried about him.'

It felt strange to hear someone else talking about John and his addiction, someone who wasn't part of the family or Kev, who was the only other person that I had told. It still felt like something that other people shouldn't know about, like we should have kept it to ourselves as a secret until it was sorted, and then we wouldn't have to tell anybody at all.

'Do you want to tell us what's going on?' Dad asked. 'Why haven't you been going to training?'

I wasn't sure if I could explain without it all sounding a bit stupid. Part of it was because I was annoyed at myself for what had happened. But a lot of it was definitely embarrassment too. Everyone who knew me – my friends, the lads in school, our neighbours – knew me as Philly, the footballer who was going to play for Dublin someday. The next Colm Doyle, isn't that what Mr O'Dea had said to me that night? Except that was all gone now, none of it was true any more, and without it, I didn't know who I was supposed to be.

I kept thinking about the happiness on Mam's face when I came home that night and she rushed out into the hall, waving the academy letter at me, or how excited Dad had been to rummage through all of the new gear that I had been sent. It had been a big deal for Colm too, and I had let all of them down by getting expelled. If I didn't go back to football, I didn't have to face it.

But I didn't say any of those things. 'I don't feel like playing any more,' I said. That was the best I could manage in answer to Dad's question.

'But you love football,' Mam said. 'That's all you've ever wanted to do.'

'Yeah, I wanted to play for Dublin, but it's all a fix. If you're from Ballymun, you have to be twice as good as everyone else just to get a fair chance in the first place. What's the point?' I really believed that was true, but then I remembered that Kev was in the academy and he seemed to be getting on okay.

'So you're giving up then?' Dad said, his voice low. 'Winners never quit and quitters never win; that's what my da used to tell me all the time.'

Colm interrupted before I had a chance to get drawn into another one of Granddad's life lessons. 'If this is about the academy, I might be able to fix it.'

'How?' I said, curious. Gerry Mangan's decision had seemed pretty final to me. I couldn't see how there was any way back.

'I rang Gerry again the other day, after your parents

told me about John, and I explained the situation to him.'

I felt my face getting hot at the mention of John's name and Gerry Mangan's in the same sentence.

'I thought it was important that he had all the facts,' Colm continued. He looked to Mam and Dad for reassurance, and I could see that they agreed. 'You shouldn't have lashed out, but I think he's having second thoughts about how he handled the whole situation. Unfortunately, the county board has some silly policy that means he can't just recall you if he changes his mind.'

If this was good news, I was still waiting for the good bit.

'But,' he said optimistically, 'Gerry is allowed to bring any new players into the academy once Féile is finished, so he'll be there with the other coaches to scout all the games, and he'll keep an eye out for you.'

'Isn't that brilliant news?' Mam said. 'You'll be able to get your place back.' All three of them seemed delighted, as though this would solve the problem, but I wasn't so sure.

'Look, Gerry understands,' Colm assured me, 'especially now that he knows what you're dealing with and how you were provoked.'

'You told him about John!' I said angrily. 'That wasn't your information to go spreading around. You're not part of this family.'

Colm looked stunned. He didn't know how to respond. Dad intervened on his behalf. 'Hang on a second now. Colm discussed it with us first, and we all agreed that telling Gerry was the right thing to do.'

'That wasn't your decision to make either,' I protested, getting more upset. 'Why do you think I changed my name the first day I went up there?'

'You did what?' Mam said.

'I told them my name was Philly McMahon. I didn't want anyone hearing the name Caffrey and realising my brother is John Caffrey, the guy with the heroin addiction.'

Mam's face fell. I hadn't planned to tell them like this – I hadn't planned to tell them at all. I shouldn't have said anything.

'They'll all know now.' I glared at Colm. 'But it doesn't matter, I won't be going back there anyway.'

'Don't be ridiculous – I'm sure Gerry won't say a word,' Dad said, but Colm looked flustered, clearly worried that he'd somehow managed to make a bad situation worse.

'I'm sorry if I've overstepped,' he said apologetically. 'I was – we were – only trying to help.'

'If you wanted to help, you wouldn't have taken the captaincy off me,' I snapped without missing a beat.

'That's enough, Philly, watch your mouth,' Dad warned, raising his voice, and then nobody spoke for a few moments. There was a lot to take in. I felt the room closing in around me, but the door was right there. If I ran, I'd be gone before any of them could stop me.

'Come up to training on Thursday,' Colm suggested eventually. 'The lads have been wondering where you're gone. You know that this weekend is the first weekend of Féile, right?'

He was trying not to sound too pushy about it. I knew that Féile would be starting shortly, but I hadn't realised that it was quite so soon.

'We've Na Fianna on Saturday,' he added, hoping that would get my attention. Na Fianna were our biggest local rival. Their home pitch was just down the road, and a lot of their players went to school with the Glasnevin lads on our team.

'You've loads of good players. Why do you care so much if I show up or not?' I said. Players stopped coming to training and dropped off the team all the time. Sometimes they came back and sometimes they didn't. But I found it hard to imagine Colm calling around to where they lived and sitting down with their parents to try to convince them.

He put his cup down and moved it over to one side. 'I'll tell you a story that I don't tell many people,' he said. 'I try not to think about it too much.

'I didn't play Féile in my year. I had a stupid disagreement with the man who was managing the team. He wanted me to play at full-back but I really wanted to play in midfield. He was trying to pick the best team, and I thought I knew better than him. I was thirteen.' He shook his head at the memory of it. 'In the end, he told me that it was up to me: I could either play at full-back or I could go and play soccer. You know how you're always listening to me talk about opportunities and good decisions. Well, that was one of the worst decisions I ever made.' He tapped his knuckles on the table. 'I was never any good at soccer.'

'Is that a real story?' I asked.

'Yep. That was nearly twenty years ago,' he said, 'and even though I went back playing the next season, and I've been very lucky to have a wonderful career since, I still regret it. You only get one Féile year, and once it was gone, it was gone, and I never got it back again.'

Mam stared at me as he told his story, waiting for me to draw a line under everything and agree to go back training, but I couldn't look her in the eye. It was obvious how much Féile meant to Colm. Not that long ago, it had been every bit as important to me, but I just didn't care about it any more.

I was determined to have the last word. If Colm didn't want me as his captain, I didn't want him as my coach; I wanted him to feel the same way that I felt.

'I'm finished with football. See you, Colm,' I said, and I turned and walked out of the room.

21

Our near miss with the guards didn't seem to bother Al and Shane at all. For a couple of weeks afterwards, any time I saw a squad car coming, I pulled my tracksuit top up to cover the bottom half of my face and dipped my head, just in case they recognised me. I'm sure it only made me look more sketchy.

One chase by a garda through the streets of Ballymun was enough for me, but it didn't stop the others from plotting and planning. The summer nights got longer, and they spent them talking about what they would do differently 'the next time'. The rest of the time we spent sitting out in the field, trying to pick a spot so that Al and Shane could have a drink and a smoke without risking running into their parents.

That's exactly what we were doing, nothing out of the ordinary, on the night that the man approached us.

'That stuff will rot your brains, lads,' he warned, arriving into the middle of our conversation without anyone noticing he was there.

'Ah, would you shut –' Al stopped mid-sentence when he looked up and saw who he was speaking to. The man was wearing an open jacket over a jumper and a shirt, with a pair of dark jeans and polished black boots. He was around the same age as Dad, if I had to guess, maybe a year or two younger.

'Tut tut tut, Alan,' he said, wagging his finger in an exaggerated way, pretending to be serious. 'Did nobody ever teach you to look before you speak? You'll get yourself in trouble.'

Al put his can down, holding it upright between his feet. I'd never heard anyone call him Alan before; even his parents called him Al. It made me strangely tense.

'Oh,' he said sheepishly. 'Sorry, I didn't see that it was you.'

The man didn't look at all familiar to me but Al obviously knew who he was.

'You're all right, Alan.' He smiled, but it was more of a grimace. 'Doesn't bother me.' And then he muttered it again to himself, the words sneaking out from under his breath. 'Doesn't bother me one bit.'

There was an uneasy pause where no one said anything. The man raised his eyebrows. 'Well, how's your da doing?' he asked.

'He's good, thanks. I'll tell him I was talking to you.'

There was something strange about the way Al was acting. It wasn't just that he was being polite. He was being overly polite, as if he was trying to make a good impression with his friendliness and manners.

'His da' – the man was talking to me and Shane now – 'is a great man, but you lads already know that, I'm sure.'

I didn't think Al really got on with his dad much. He was an angry man who seemed to do far too much shouting and roaring, even over little things, but now wasn't the time to point that out. I smiled and nodded and Shane did the same.

'Young Mark too,' he said. 'He's a hard worker, that lad. He has his head screwed on.' He tapped his finger against the side of his head for emphasis, and even in the dark, I could see the jagged scar that ran the length of his jawline, faded with the years.

When he mentioned Mark, I wondered if he was talking about Al's uncle. He must have been. Whoever this man was, he seemed to know a lot of people – Al's family, at the very least. He didn't seem to be in much of a rush. He took a lighter out of his pocket and started flicking it so that it sparked but didn't light, and he whistled a little tune to himself.

'Anyway, Alan,' he said after a few moments, 'seeing as I've bumped into you, I have a little job that you might like to do for me.'

Al jumped to attention – 'Of course, yeah. I'd be happy to help if I can,' he said – but I was beginning to think it wasn't an accident that he'd happened to find the three of us sitting there.

'Very good, very good,' the man said. 'It won't take too long but it's important so I'll need someone I can trust, which is why I'm asking you.'

Al's chest stuck out a bit further when he heard that.

'Now, normally, it would be about two hundred euro for the job …'

If I hadn't already been sitting down, I would have fallen over. Shane's eyes lit up.

'But, sure, seeing as it's you and you'd be doing me a favour, I think I can make it three hundred this time around.'

The three of us were hanging on his every word now. That was the type of money you could spend for months and still have change left over.

'Actually, now that I think of it,' he said, sizing up me and Shane but talking to Al, 'it might be more of a two-man job, or even a three-man job, so bring your friends with you if you like. The same deal for all of you – three hundred euro each – and if it all goes well, it shouldn't be more than twenty minutes' work.'

Shane looked the way I felt, practically giddy at the thought of all that money and unable to believe our good luck. The two of us were too stunned to speak but Al accepted on all our behalfs. 'We'd be happy to. What do you need from us?'

The man took a phone out of his pocket and looked at it while he thought about the question for a moment. 'It's a quarter past ten,' he said. 'Meet me back here at the same time tomorrow night and I'll give you the instructions.'

We watched him walk away – in the opposite direction to the shops, I noticed – and waited until he was gone before bursting into excitement.

'Holy … did he say three hundred each?' Shane said in total disbelief. He cracked open his last can in celebration.

'Who's your man?' I asked Al, but he was distracted and he wasn't listening to me.

'What?'

'Who's your da's rich mate and what does he do if he's offering us' – I did the maths quickly – 'nine hundred euro for a few minutes' work?'

Al gave me one of those looks he sometimes gave me, like he couldn't understand how he was friends with someone who asked such ridiculous questions. 'You don't know who that was?' He sounded nervous, not excited.

'No. Do you know who it was?' I asked Shane, getting a bit defensive. He shook his head as he swallowed his beer.

Al's face dropped as he looked at us. 'That was Charlie Hanlon.'

As soon as the words left Al's mouth, my heart sank. 'What?' I panicked, hoping that Al was on the wind-up. 'Tell me you're messing.'

'Why would I mess about something like that?' Al said, and there wasn't even a hint of a joke in his voice. I realised that there was no such thing as an easy €300. We were in way over our heads.

'How do you know Charlie Hanlon?'

'Dad is good mates with him,' Al explained. 'Well, they were good mates when they were younger. Dad doesn't really like talking about it but he told me one night when he came in from the pub.'

'Tell us,' I said impatiently, and Al held up his hand, telling me to settle down.

'The two of you aren't to tell anyone this, you promise?'

'Of course, yeah.'

He hesitated.

'We won't say a word, Al, honestly.'

'All right, all right. This was years ago. Dad said he wasn't getting much work around the time when Mam was pregnant with me, and they were a bit stuck for money, so him and Charlie ended up doing a job together. He didn't tell me what it was, but whatever happened, they got caught. Dad was the one who took the fall for it and ended up in jail, and Charlie got off scot-free.'

Al's dad was a painter and decorator, but Al had never told us that he had been in jail. 'How long was he in for?' Shane asked.

'Four years,' Al said. 'I think that's probably why him and Mam are always fighting. He was in jail when I was born, and he wasn't around at all until I was three, and Mam had to mind me by herself all of that time.'

'And they're still mates now, are they?' I said.

'Yeah. Well, I think Charlie made sure that Mam had everything she needed for me when I was born and I was little. I suppose if he had been nicked that time with Dad, or instead of Dad, he probably wouldn't be the most powerful gangster in the city now. So he was paying Dad back for that, and he still drops over to the flat a couple of times a year, which is how I know him.'

I tried to think back to some things that had happened when I was nine; four years seemed like a long time, and a very long time to be in prison. We were in a serious situation.

'What do you think he'll want us to do?' I wondered out loud.

'I'm not sure, but we can't really say no to him, can we?' Shane said.

Al drummed his fingers off the side of his can. 'I don't really have a choice, but you lads do, I suppose.'

Everything about the situation screamed at us to run a million miles, yet we were still sitting there talking about it as if there was a decision to be made. All the stories I'd heard about Charlie Hanlon ran through my head on a loop. Surely he hadn't got to where he was by trusting random teenagers that he met out in the field with important jobs? Whatever he had in mind, it had to be something straightforward, something that he expected the three of us to be able to do for him. It couldn't be that difficult.

I wondered what Kev would make of it all if he was here – but he wasn't. All I had to go on were Al's and Shane's reactions. They both seemed scared too, but not scared enough to say no. If they went, I'd follow.

'Three hundred euro is a lot of money,' I pointed out, wondering what exactly would be a suitable price if we did put ourselves in harm's way.

'Maybe we should just see what he says tomorrow,'

Shane suggested, and Al seemed relieved that we weren't going to leave him in this mess by himself.

And that's how we agreed that we would meet one of Dublin's most notorious criminals to do a job for him.

22

left Al and Shane and walked the long way home, up past the Towers, in case John was there and I spotted him. Lots of people were dotted around in little groups but there was no sign of him, so I didn't hang around. When I got closer to home, I heard someone calling me.

'Here, Philly, stall it.'

I turned around. It was Kev. I had been avoiding him, but I'd never been as happy to see him as I was then. My heart was still rattling so hard that I felt it all the way up in my neck. I had to tell him about what had just happened, about Charlie Hanlon. He'd know what to do.

'What's the story?' he said, walking over to join me. 'Where have you been? Every time I knock up to the flat, you're not there.'

We hadn't really spoken since school had finished because I knew he'd try to convince me to go back playing football. And I was happy for Kev – I really was – but every time I saw him, I would be reminded that he was in the academy and that I had made a mess of it.

'Ah, I'm just out hanging around. I haven't seen you much either,' I said, playing dumb. 'You must be busy with everything going on.'

'Yeah, it's great.' I could see he had loads that he wanted to tell me. We were used to spending all day, every day together, and now we hadn't seen each other in weeks.

'Is everything all right?' he asked. 'Are things all right at home, I mean?'

'Yeah, it's grand.'

'It's just that you're acting really weird at the minute. It's like you've disappeared. What's going on? Why did you stop coming to training?'

'Dunno, I just lost interest.'

Kev knew there was more to the story than I was

telling him. There had to be. I could see that he was hurt – we always told each other everything – but he didn't push me on it.

'Did Colm call around to yours to speak to you?' he asked.

'Yeah, maybe two weeks ago. I think he was trying to get my mam and dad to convince me to go back, but we ended up having a bit of a row instead. I doubt he wants me back now.'

'I wouldn't be so sure.'

'What do you mean?'

'He asked me to keep an eye out for you and to talk to you if I saw you. He didn't want me to go knocking on your door, though. He said to make it look like I'd just met you by chance – I probably wasn't supposed to tell you that bit,' he said, and we both laughed. He still knew how to get a laugh out of me, even if things were a bit strange between us.

'I've been hanging around here most nights waiting to see you but you're never around. Come up to training tomorrow night, come on.'

He wasn't asking me because Colm had sent him. He was asking because he was my friend.

'Nobody cares about what happened with the academy,' Kev continued. 'Nobody cares that you've gone missing for a few weeks. The only thing that anyone's worried about now is Féile, and how we're going to win it, and we need you for that. Everyone will be delighted to see you.'

The story Colm had told me was still stuck in my head, and it bounced back to the front again when Kev mentioned Féile. Would I still regret it in 20 years if I didn't go back?

'How many matches have you played?' I asked.

'Three so far. We won all of our group games so we've two weeks off now, and then we're into the semis against Vincent's, and the other semi is Crokes against Christopher's.'

'It sounds like you're doing fine without me so.'

'Don't be stupid. You know you're the best player on the team, and you're our captain as well. I don't even want to be captain. I told Colm I was only doing it until you came back.'

Kev knew me long enough to know that I could be a bit stubborn – more than a bit, if we're being honest – so he left it there and changed the subject. 'How's John doing?'

I shrugged my shoulders. Truth was, I didn't really know.

'He's home at the moment, though, isn't he?' Kev said. 'I saw him the other day when he was helping Mrs O'Dea.'

'Helping her with what?' I said, puzzled. I hadn't a

clue what he was talking about.

'Oh,' Kev said, as if he somehow expected me to already know. 'She was coming back from the shops the other day and she nearly got hit by a car. Some lad flew around the corner and didn't see her. He slammed on the brakes and beeped, but Mrs O'Dea got such a fright that she dropped the shopping bags in the middle of the road and all of her stuff went everywhere.'

I had a picture in my head of smashed eggs and tins of beans rolling off and poor Mrs O'Dea scrambling around in the middle of it all.

'That dope in the car just revved the engine and drove around her and sped off,' Kev said, shaking his head. 'He never stopped to see if she was okay or anything. I was playing football out in the field and I heard all the noise and saw her chasing after the stuff.

'I was going over to help her, but before I got there, John had seen it happen too and was straight over. He stopped the traffic so he could pick up all her stuff and pack it back into the bags, and he got her purse out of the middle of the road for her and then carried it all back up to the flat.'

My mind immediately jumped to all sorts of bad conclusions when Kev mentioned Mrs O'Dea's purse, and then I got upset for even allowing myself to think those things.

'He was gone before I got a chance to talk to him,' Kev said, 'so I was just wondering how he's doing. Anyway, look, I'll see you tomorrow – seven o'clock in Poppintree Park.'

Just thinking about the following day, and whatever it was that Charlie Hanlon had planned, gave me a shiver. Now was my last chance to tell Kev about it, to see what he thought, to ask for his help. I thought of what to say, and then I changed my mind and said nothing at all.

'Training? Sound, yeah, I'll think about it,' I said.

'What's there to think about?'

A lot, I thought to myself. There's a lot to think about.

—

I thought about it the whole next day, and at six o'clock, when I should have been checking my boots and packing my bag, I went to meet Al and Shane instead. Charlie Hanlon had said a quarter past ten but I needed to get out of the flat. I knew Kev would knock up for me so we could walk over to training together, the way that we had always done, and I didn't want to be at home when he called. I didn't want him to try to convince me. And I didn't want to have to tell him where I was going instead.

I met Al and Shane outside the eight-storeys and

we walked around to the pub to play a few games of pool to pass the time. None of us spoke much. Not knowing what we would be asked to do was the worst part because that meant that, for now, everything was a possibility; if the lads were anything like me, their imaginations were being annoyingly creative.

Shane pulled a bar stool over to the side of the table so he could sit and watch without getting in the way while Al and I played first. He was messing around with the plastic triangle used for racking the balls, throwing it up in the air and catching it, until he dropped it with a clatter.

'Stop fidgeting – you're making me nervous,' Al said angrily. 'You lads go home if you want to. I can do this by myself.'

But he didn't mean it. I knew he was glad that we were there with him.

We played pool until the pub started to get a bit busier, men and women coming in for a drink after their dinner, and there was a bit of a queue of people looking to use the table. We played one last game and we left. It was still early, just before eight o'clock, and far too bright for someone like Charlie Hanlon to be seen instructing three kids about a job.

Al wanted to go to Macari's so we walked over there and waited outside while he went in and got a fish box and chips. I had a few euro in my pocket but I wasn't hungry, although I still nicked a couple of chips on him when he offered. The smell of them was too good to resist.

Al was starving but he took his time eating, just so that he had something to do, and then we slowly walked back up towards the Towers, to the place where we had been told to meet. The lads smoked while we waited, passing the time, but they hadn't brought any cans with them. Shane had a watch, kept checking it, updating us with the time every two minutes – seven minutes past, nine minutes past, eleven minutes past – until I had to ask him to stop.

But four minutes after Shane's last update, at the exact time he said he would meet us, a black 4x4 Jeep pulled up across the road and Charlie Hanlon stepped out of the driver's seat.

He was by himself again, and dressed almost identically to the way he had been the previous evening. His hair was slicked back with a lot of hair gel, shining like he had just got out of the shower and split into lines where he had run his comb through it. He wore two thick gold rings, one on either hand. This time, there was no friendly greeting, no chit-chat, no asking about Al's family. Everything seemed a lot more business like. Professional.

'All three of you,' he said with a bit of surprise. 'Very

good. You have good friends, Alan.' He didn't ask us our names or who we were. There was an urgency in his voice as he gave us our instructions. 'This is very simple, lads. A man is on his way here now with an important parcel for me. He's expecting to meet one of my friends to deliver it but that friend is' – he paused, which sounded very dodgy – 'unfortunately unavailable this evening, which is why it's great that you lads are kindly available to help me.

'He'll be arriving up outside number twenty-one in Plunkett Tower in half an hour, at a quarter to eleven, and he'll be on time. I need you lads to go there and meet him when he arrives and collect that parcel for me. Tell him I sent you. You understand, do you?'

We all nodded silently. I didn't know what was going through Al's and Shane's heads, but I was too afraid to say anything.

'You boys know Daz, I'm sure, do you?' he said. 'Daz Kearns?'

'Yeah, we do,' Al answered. The bad feeling that I already had about all of this was getting worse.

'Good. I can't stick around this evening,' he said, smiling like he was laughing at a joke that only he understood, 'but Daz will meet you back here in an hour, at a quarter past eleven sharp, so you need to take good care of the parcel until he comes to collect it from you. Don't let it out of your sight,' he warned, 'and do not open it.'

It sounded simple. For a moment, I convinced myself that the three of us had massively overreacted, until Charlie Hanlon pursed his lips and spoke again.

'Oh,' he said, as if he'd suddenly just remembered, 'there's just one other small detail that you need to know, lads. I need you to get that parcel for me tonight, but this man who is delivering it, I'm sure he's expecting to be paid for it. That's the tricky part. We've had a bit of a disagreement so I've decided to – how should I say it? – withhold the payment for now.'

He stepped towards us, close enough that I could see the creases on his forehead. My mouth was as dry as a bone from the nerves.

'He'll be expecting you to give him the money before he hands over the parcel,' he explained, 'but you won't have any money, so you'll need to convince him to, eh, do what's good for him.'

I wasn't sure exactly what he meant until he reached inside his jacket and pulled out three small black objects. With a flick, he opened one of them, and the steel blade of the knife glistened in the night's light.

'I brought you one each,' he said, holding them out in our direction.

I froze at the sight of them. These were serious knives

236

– they weren't for show. And if he was giving them to us, he was expecting us to need them.

'Don't worry,' he tried to reassure us, flicking the knife closed again. 'This is just for a little extra protection.' He held the knives towards us on the open palm of his hand.

Al took the three knives and passed one to Shane, who took it and stuffed it into his pocket quickly. I didn't want any part of this. It was way too dangerous. We didn't know anything about this man we were being sent to meet, only that we were effectively being asked to rob him at knife point on behalf of the biggest criminal in Dublin. Anything could go wrong, and if something did, you could be sure that nobody would come rushing to help us. Anybody passing by would be smart enough to mind their own business. And now it was time for me to mind mine.

I looked at the knife in Al's hand. I wondered who had held it before, what they had done with it. Who they had hurt. I pushed his hand away as he offered me the knife. 'I – I can't.' I had to force the words out. 'I can't do it. I'm sorry.'

'What are you doing?' Al whispered, a mix of panic and frustration, but there was nothing he could say or do that would convince me to stay.

I took a few steps away so I could run if any of them

tried to stop me. Shane froze and didn't react at all. His hand was still in his pocket, gripping the plastic of the knife. If there was a way out, he would have taken it too, but Al was committed and Shane stood with him.

'Sorry that I can't help you,' I said half-heartedly to Charlie Hanlon. I waited for him to try and stop me. Now that I knew what the job was, he might think that I was a problem, that I might tell someone and wreck his plans. But I wouldn't tell anyone. I just wanted to get out of there. I turned and walked away, slowly at first and then a little bit faster.

'Philly, wait, would you?' Al called after me, but there was nothing to wait for. Once I was far enough away, I broke into a sprint, and I didn't stop sprinting until I was home again.

23

When I got home, John was there by himself. He was lying on the couch, stretched out along the full length of it, with MTV turned down low in the background, and he sat up when he saw me come in. Something about him seemed different. He still looked like a shadow, but somewhere in there, I caught a spark of his old energy and life that I thought the heroin had drained away forever.

And for the first time in a long time, I was glad to see him. Really glad to see him.

The whole way home, all I could think of was how stupid I had to be to go with Al and Shane. What if I had upset Charlie Hanlon's plans and the lads told him where I lived? What if he came looking for me here? I should have walked away as soon as Al mentioned his name, and I never should have agreed to meet him a second time. The knot in my stomach tightened; I should have tried to convince Al and Shane to leave with me. I was okay for the moment, I hoped, but they were in real danger now. The worst thing was, I wasn't sure if they fully realised it.

I was glad to see that Mam and Dad were out, but John would understand. He'd know the right thing to do. The moment he sat up and looked at me, he knew straight away that something was wrong.

I needed his help. He moved over on the couch and I sat down beside him and, for a moment, I forgot about everything except for the trouble that I was in. I told John what had happened, and when I mentioned the name Charlie Hanlon, he grabbed me by the collar of my tracksuit top.

'What are you doing talking to Charlie Hanlon?' The fear in his eyes did nothing to reassure me that this was all going to be okay in the end.

'I didn't know it was him,' I said. 'I'd never even seen him before. Al only told us who he was after he had left.'

'Where are Al and Shane now?'

'I dunno – I'd say they're gone up to Plunkett to wait for that man to arrive. Do you think they're all right?' My brain was on a rollercoaster. 'What are we going to do? When will Mam and Dad be home? Maybe we should call the guards or something?'

A rush of energy hit me, and in the next instant, it vanished and pure worry poured through me. I felt like I was running and not quite able to catch my breath. I was panicking. John jumped up off the couch, and for a moment, I thought he was about to run up to the Towers to drag the lads out of there before it was too late.

'Sit down, would you? Where are you going?' I knew he meant well if he was thinking that he could help the lads, but if he went, I'd have to go with him, and I really didn't want to do that.

'That man is dangerous, do you hear me?' he said. 'I don't want you ever going near him again, for any reason.'

'We have to do something, John,' I begged him. 'Please. Help me.'

John sat back down beside me. 'All right, it's okay, it'll be grand, don't worry, just calm down for a second,' he said, doing his best to reassure me before I lost the plot completely, then he stood back up and started pacing up and down again. He couldn't sit still.

'You were right to get out of there. I'm sure Al and Shane will be smart enough to figure it out.'

That was all I wanted: for someone to tell me I had done the right thing – eventually – even if there was no guarantee that everything was going to be okay.

John's tone changed again. 'Were you not supposed to be at training?' he said, connecting the dots. 'It's Thursday.'

That was how little we had spoken in the last few months. I hadn't been interested in celebrating with him when I was picked for the academy, and I hadn't told him that I had been expelled or that I had stopped training with Kickhams.

'Yeah, there was training earlier,' I said, 'but I didn't go.'

'Why not? Kev knocked up for you but you weren't here so I told him you must have gone on ahead, and he went off looking for you. What's going on?'

'I dunno, I've just stopped going the last few weeks. I'm not that interested any more,' I said, and I went right back to the start, to the day of the academy trials, and told him the whole story.

'So that's it then?' he said when I was finished. 'You're giving up. No more football?'

'Maybe, yeah, I dunno …'

'That's the most ridiculous thing I've ever heard,' he said, cutting me off. 'Don't be such an idiot.'

I hadn't expected such a strong reaction from him. I wanted to explain myself better so he could see where I was coming from and understand, but I let him speak instead.

'Football, being on that Ballymun team with all of your mates, that dream you have of playing for Dublin – you don't know how lucky you are to have all that stuff,' he said. 'And now you're telling me you want to throw it all away over something stupid? I didn't think you were that much of a dope.'

The truth in his words hit me hard, but his disappointment hit me harder, and it set me off. He had no right to sit there giving me a lecture. 'Why do you even care?' I lashed out. 'You've been gone for months. I might as well not even have a brother.'

John's face crumpled. He stood up and walked to the other side of the room. Then he said something that stopped everything. 'You know, I was your age when all of this started.'

I didn't fully know what he meant. 'What, you were thirteen when …?' I started the thought but I couldn't finish it, and left it for him instead.

'When I started taking drugs, yeah,' he said, and he breathed a long, heavy sigh. 'I was fourteen when I tried heroin for the first time. Mam and Dad don't even know that.'

I couldn't believe what he was telling me. I didn't want

to believe it. I tried to think back to when I was six or seven, and all of the happy times we had together since then, up until the last few months. He was my big brother, the one person I always looked up to, my hero. It just didn't make sense that he had been using drugs all of that time.

'How did that even happen?' I said. I didn't want to know and, at the same time, I did.

John switched the TV off and started a story that I'm sure he never expected to have to tell me. 'It was a mistake. We were kids and we were bored. We didn't know what we were doing. We were just hanging around. There were four of us that day – the first day. It was me and Wayne Mac and Ciarán and Daz Kearns.'

I thought about the names as he mentioned them. I never knew Wayne Mac, even though Mam was good friends with Claire, his mam. All I could think of was the day of his funeral last year, surrounded by people in floods of tears and every one of them seemed to have a funny story to tell about him.

'Is Ciarán bad with it too?' I asked. He was one of the lads that I knew well from hanging around in the field with John. I knew he smoked joints sometimes, but I never imagined that he was using heroin too.

'No, actually,' John said. 'I don't know how it happened, but his da caught him later on that day and found out. They moved him out of school and sent him down to stay with his aunt and uncle in Galway for a couple of years. That's why he wasn't around for so long,' he explained, 'but, sure, you were probably too young back then to remember any of that.'

'How did he get caught and you didn't?'

John smiled but it was a sad smile. 'He never told his da that we were with him – he didn't want to get us into trouble – and then he was gone to Galway two days later. If he had ratted me out, I'm sure his da would have told Mam and Dad, and then ...'

And then maybe we wouldn't be having this conversation, I thought.

'The four of us went up to the Towers,' he said. 'The lifts used to work back in those days – most of the time, anyway; they weren't always broken like they are now – but we knew a little trick to make them stop working, and then we could get into them and lock ourselves in.'

He talked me through what they did: they got into the lift as normal and waited for the doors to close, but didn't press a button to go anywhere. There were two sets of doors on the Ballymun lifts, one on the outside and one on the inside, and if you forced the inner doors open from the inside and wedged them open – with a bit of a stick or something – it tricked the lift into thinking it was broken. If anyone pressed the button to try to call it, it wouldn't move. It just stayed there stuck, with the lads inside it, until they took the stick out; there was nothing anyone else could do.

The first time it happened, none of the people who lived in the block of flats knew what was happening, but over time, they realised the lads were doing it deliberately and using it for drinking and smoking and whatever else they were getting up to.

'I didn't have a clue what was going on,' John continued. 'I thought we were just going to go up and smoke a joint or something. We couldn't do it out on the blocks. We were only kids. I was afraid Mam or Dad would see me – they'd kill me. I don't think any of us knew what we were doing.

'Daz asked us if we wanted to do some "H" with him, but I didn't know what H was or what he was talking about. Ciarán took the first hit of it. He said it was liquid hash. We all did it then. I didn't even know it was heroin I was taking.'

'No,' I said in utter disbelief, barely able to get the word out. 'No, no, no, that can't be true. Tell me that's not true. You took heroin and you didn't even know what it was?' I shoved him in the chest and pushed him back into the side of the couch. 'You've ruined everything, and now you're trying to tell me that you didn't even know what you were doing.'

I went to shove him again, but this time he caught

my arms and held them. Even though he was skinny and weak, he was still stronger than me. 'Stop, would you? Calm down. Please,' he said. I pulled my arms free from him and collapsed into the middle of the couch and started crying.

'I'm thirteen,' I reminded him through the tears. 'I know never to even think about going near heroin. I've known that nearly since I could walk. How could you have been so stupid?'

That was really what upset me the most about his story. I hated John for using heroin; I hated him because he knew all of the hurt and the pain it was causing, to himself and to us, and he still chose to do it. But I never knew how it had started – he had made a mistake, a stupid, bored mistake. He was the same age as me and it had changed his life forever. It didn't seem fair.

'I know it was stupid,' he said. 'I know.' He looked like he was about to start crying too. 'Look at what it's after doing to me. I know you think I keep on taking it because I want to, that I could stop if I tried hard enough. All I want is to get better. I'm trying so hard.'

'I don't understand, though,' I said. 'What is it doing? Why aren't you able to stop?'

John thought for a second so he could try to find the right words. 'I don't really know how to explain it to you,' he admitted. 'At the start, I kept taking it because it was a good buzz and I thought it would make me happy. And I thought that I'd be able to stop whenever I wanted, so I didn't think it was doing any harm. But then I needed more of it, and more of it, and now I'm in so much pain if I don't take it. I need it just to drown out the voices in my head. I need it just to forget.'

I had been to so many anti-drug rallies and marches, so many funerals of young people that Mam or Dad or my sisters or John knew, but I still didn't fully understand the evil in the world that allowed something like heroin to exist in the first place. It had ruined him from the inside out.

'I was stupid,' he said. 'So, so stupid. I made a mistake – I made a lot of mistakes – but I was fourteen. I didn't know any better. But there was no way back. Once you have a drug addiction, nobody wants to know you. You're a junkie. It's such a horrible word – it's like you're not even human any more. Everyone thinks you're dirt.'

He rubbed the corner of his eye. 'You're my brother and you wouldn't sit at the same table and eat dinner with me. You wouldn't even speak to me.'

When I was pushing him away like that, or when Mam and Dad put him out of the flat, I thought that was what we needed to do to help him, that we needed to make him choose between our love and the heroin and that our love would win. But I didn't know anything about how powerful it was, how deep its claws were, and I never appreciated how isolated he had felt.

'I'm sorry,' I said.

'Look, I'm not blaming you or saying it's your fault, but imagine what that must be like. The only people who really understand are other people who have an addiction. They know how it feels to have a countdown clock on your life, when it seems like the rest of the world is just waiting for you to die and stop being an inconvenience.'

We talked and talked, and I realised I knew nothing about what John was going through. It wasn't as simple as choosing to have an addiction. It was never that simple. And if the only connection he felt was when he was with other people struggling in the same way, how was he ever going to get away from it?

'Mam told me that she's trying to find someone who can help you,' I said. 'She spoke to some man about getting you a bed in a rehab centre?'

'Yeah, she did. I was ready to go in last week, but then they told her they couldn't take me for some reason. I've been thinking about it, though, and I think that maybe I should go to London.'

'Why London?'

'I don't know if I'll ever get better if I stay here. I know too many people. It's too easy to fall back into bad habits. I could get a fresh start over in London, you know?'

I nodded. That made sense.

'Mam rang around a few places, and she found a rehab centre that will have a spot for me in a few weeks.' He had the plan all mapped out already. 'I'll probably get the boat over,' he continued, and he sounded almost excited as he told me. 'And then if I go over there for six months and get away from it all, I'll be able to come home again so we can all have Christmas together. That would be nice, wouldn't it?'

It sounded amazing, but I didn't want to get my hopes up.

John picked up on my hesitation. 'I'll do it – I promise you I will,' he said. 'But you need to promise me something too. Go back playing football and get back into that Dublin academy. I've made enough mistakes for both of us, so learn from them. You dodged a big one tonight, but what about the next time, when there's no knives, when there's more money, when you're bored, when you're desperate. What are you going to do then?'

He was making more sense than I had heard him make in a long, long time. I knew he was right.

'Okay,' I said. 'I'll go back.'

'No, promise me. Say "I promise".' He held out his hand for me to shake, and when I did, he pulled me into a hug.

'I promise, John.'

We were still talking when Mam and Dad came home a few minutes later.

'Oh good,' Mam said. 'You're both here.'

She seemed flustered and very relieved to see us, and I could tell by the look on her face that something bad was after happening.

'Yeah, we're just talking,' I said. 'What's the matter? Is something wrong?'

'There's an ambulance up outside the Towers,' Mam said as she sat down on the arm of the chair, still wearing her coat. 'We were just walking by on our way home and we overheard someone saying that two teenagers had been attacked and needed to go to hospital. Something about a fight in the flats. We didn't stop to see what was going on. I was just worried that something might have happened to one of you. Thank God you're both here safe.'

Mam was still talking as I ran out of the room. I burst through the front door, leaving it swinging behind me, and their shouts followed me down the stairs and into the night. The blue lights were still flashing as I ran towards them. As I got closer, I could see a crowd of people gathered around and two guards starting to take statements. The back doors of the ambulance were open, and as I looked in, there, lying on stretchers on either side while paramedics tended to them, were Al and Shane.

24

Al and Shane weren't allowed to have visitors in hospital for the first few days. It was family only, the doctors insisted. When I finally got in to see them, they were on two different wards. Al's was on the first floor so I went there first. It was his eye that I noticed first, black and purple and yellow, puffed out and completely swollen shut. His face had taken all the damage.

'How did you get in here?' he asked, looking up with his good eye as he spotted me coming in the door.

'I told the woman at reception that I was your brother,' I said, handing him a little paper bag with a bottle of Coke and a Twix.

He laughed, then stopped suddenly, wincing in pain. 'Don't do that,' he said. 'It hurts too much.'

He looked a little like a mummy, with more bandages and plasters covering his face than skin. He had a broken nose and a broken cheekbone as well.

When I went to see Shane, judging by his face, you would barely know that he had been in a fight at all. There wasn't a mark on him, but he was plugged in to all sorts of machines and monitors beside his bed, beeping and flashing with numbers and lines that neither of us understood. He had two cracked ribs, and one of them had splintered and punctured his lung. He lifted up the side of his hospital gown to show me the bandage wrapped around his chest.

'They had to make a hole and stick a big tube in there,' he said, pointing to his side up underneath his arm, 'otherwise my lungs would have filled up with all sorts of stuff and I wouldn't have been able to breathe.'

One of the paramedics at the scene found the knives near where the lads had been beaten up and said it was a miracle that neither of them had been stabbed or slashed. They both had to stay in hospital for a few days but, other than that, the doctors said they would both be fine.

I was delighted to hear that. From the moment that Mam came home that night and told us what had happened, I felt guilty about walking away and leaving them. Every time I thought of it – which was a lot – I couldn't get rid of the feeling that it was partly my fault they had been beaten up and were in hospital, that I could have stayed and somehow talked them out of it. They never even got their €300 in the end. When they didn't get the package, the message from Charlie Hanlon was that they were lucky not to be getting a second beating from one of his men.

—

The rehab centre phoned to say that John's place was ready sooner than expected, and so, less than two weeks after he first told me about his plan, he moved over to London. Mam wanted to go with him, just to make sure that he got there and got settled in without any problems, but he told her this was something that he had to do by himself. It would be easier for everyone this way, he insisted.

On the morning he left, he wrapped me in another one of his big bear hugs and said goodbye. 'I'm going to get better, and I'm going to be home soon,' he said as he let me go. 'No excuses.'

'No excuses,' I said, and we both knew that applied to me as much as it did to him.

On my first night back at training, I left home an hour early and, instead of going to the park, I went straight to Colm's house. He was still there when I knocked, packing all the gear into the boot of his car and getting ready to leave. I didn't want to just show up at training again and try to pretend that nothing had ever happened. I wanted to apologise to him. Properly.

I'd spent all afternoon working out what I wanted to say, practising in my head, so that he knew that I was really sorry, but he didn't want to make a big fuss out of it at all.

'I know that I let the lads down and I –'

'Stop.' He held up his hand. 'It's great to have you back. Come on, give me a hand throwing the rest of this stuff into the car and then jump into the front – I'll give you a lift down.'

'Okay. Anyway, I'm sorry,' I said. I needed to at least say that much, and Colm smiled and nodded to let me know that I didn't need to say any more.

I didn't realise how much I had missed training until I got up to the park and put my boots on and the rest of the lads started to arrive.

'You're back?' Jimmy said, coming over to give me a thump on the arm. 'We were wondering where you were gone.'

'I couldn't let you all go and win Féile without me, now, could I?'

'Nah, that sounds like a job for the Bash Brothers all right,' he agreed. 'It's good to have you back.'

I got the same reaction from everybody. Kev was right – nobody cared that I had been missing; they were all just delighted to see that I was back again. He was one of the last to arrive, five minutes before training was due to start.

'Nice one for telling me you were leaving,' he said sarcastically. 'I was knocking on your door for the last ten minutes to see where you were, and nobody answered. I thought you were after doing a runner again.'

'Oh yeah, sorry.' I had completely forgotten he would be calling up for me, and I hadn't told him I was going to leave a bit early to speak with Colm.

'Anyway, thank God you're finally back. Any time I'm late, I normally tell Colm that it was your fault.'

'You what?'

'Nah, I'm only buzzing with you.' He chuckled. 'I missed you, pal. Now, go on and get warmed up, would you?' he said, giving me a friendly shove. 'We don't want you pulling that dodgy hamstring again on your first night back.'

Everything just felt normal. It was good to be back. As I jogged over to the others to do a few stretches, I felt like I was back where I belonged.

There was a different energy to the team, and after being away for so long, I could see it clearly. Training was as intense as I had ever seen it – Tuesday, Thursday, Tuesday, Thursday – and every single player was training their socks off. But it was fun and exciting and there was a giddiness too. We had imagined Féile for so long, we'd been thinking about what it would be like to be in this position as one of the final four teams in the county, and now we were finally there. Colm was right. If I had missed it, I would have regretted it forever.

On the night of our last session before the semi-final against St Vincent's, everyone seemed so focused. Between Colm's first whistle and his last whistle, it was so important that every drill, every exercise, was done to the highest possible level. I could tell that we felt unstoppable as a group; that, whatever happened, we would find a way to win; that nobody was going to beat us.

I woke up earlier than normal on the morning of the match, even though it was an afternoon game and we weren't going to meet until one o'clock. I lay in bed for a while, thinking about Vincent's and the last time we had played them, trying to remember who their best players were and what they were like. Colm hadn't named his starting team yet, so I had no idea if I would be playing or not, but even if I wasn't, I might think of some little detail that could help someone else.

I got up eventually. The door into Mam and Dad's bedroom was open, and when I looked in, the bed was made and they were gone. They both had to work, but they had gone in early so they could be home in time for throw-in. I went into the kitchen and, a few minutes later, Kellie heard me banging around and got up and came in to me.

'You're up early,' she said, rubbing her eyes.

'Yeah, I couldn't really sleep.'

'I'll make some breakfast,' she said, and she put a pot of porridge on for the two of us. She made herself a cup of coffee while she was waiting and poured me a glass of orange juice.

'John rang last night when you were out,' she said. 'Mam and Dad told me to tell you.'

'Really? How's he getting on?' I hadn't spoken to him since he had left.

'Good,' she said, giving the pot a stir as it started to bubble. 'It sounds like he's getting on great with his treatment programme. He says he likes it and he's after making a few friends in the group.'

'That's brilliant. What's the place he's living in like?'

'He never mentioned, actually. He was more interested in asking about you than telling us any of his own news.' She made a big show out of rolling her eyes so that I knew she wasn't actually annoyed. 'He knew your match was on today so he said he'd try to ring again when he can to see what the score was. I think he really would have loved to be here to go with us.'

'What do you think the story is with his treatment? Like, if we win today, do you think there's any chance he'd be able to come home for a few days for the final?'

'I'm not sure.' She shrugged. 'I suppose it depends on how strict they are in the rehab place. It'd be great if he could, though. He sounds like he's doing really well, and it'd be nice to see him again for a few days. I miss him.'

'I know, yeah, me too.'

She passed me over a bowl, the steam still rising off the top of the porridge. 'Here, eat that while it's hot.'

It felt like one o'clock would never come. I went outside for a while and kicked a ball off the wall, just to pass a bit of time, and even though Kev knocked a bit earlier than usual, at about half twelve, I was ready to go. We had won the toss to see where the match would be played, and Poppintree Park was already buzzing by the time we got there. We stopped for a minute to watch one of the football matches that was on, Willows against somebody else, before we spotted Colm. He was off to the side, setting up an area for us to warm up in while we waited for all of the other games to finish.

When the time came for him to finally name the team, I suddenly understood why I had been on edge all morning. I was excited, of course, but I was nervous – not because of the game, but because I wasn't sure whether or not I would be picked. Normally I could pick the number three jersey out of the pile and put it on before Colm had said a word, but this was different, and as he took his notebook out of his pocket and read through the names in the full-back line, I wasn't on it.

I sat and waited while he handed out the jerseys to all of the players who were starting, and then he threw me one of the last few left in the bag. I turned it over to look at the number on the back: 19.

'Be ready if I need you,' he said.

'I will,' I said. I had no right to be disappointed, but a little piece of me was. I forced those thoughts out of my head and went out to join the others in the warm-up.

As we gathered around for the final team-talk on the sideline, the referee gave two short, sharp blasts on his whistle.

'Captains, please,' he called. Kev was standing beside me. He nudged me with his arm, and when I looked to him, he motioned for me to go in as captain. I was confused, but Kev motioned over towards where the ref was standing again.

'Go. You go,' he said under his breath, trying not to make a scene in front of the rest of the team.

'What do you mean?' I said. 'I'm not even starting.'

'It doesn't matter. You're the captain of this team. I was only subbing in while you were away.'

'Ballymun captain, please,' the ref called again. The Vincent's captain was already standing alongside him. Kev noticed as I glanced in Colm's direction, unsure what he would say if he saw me going in for the toss.

'I spoke to him already,' Kev said. 'I told him you should be the captain and I was giving it back to you. It's grand. Now go,' he said, pushing me, 'or else he'll hate us before he's even thrown the ball in.'

By the time the referee did throw it in a few minutes later, a big crowd had gathered to watch. I looked around and saw Mam, Dad, June, Lindy and Kellie all standing further down on the sideline. Lindy spotted me and gave me a thumbs up, and I waved back.

We tore into Vincent's from the very first minute, and by the middle of the first half, we were already six points up and in control. Taz scored two goals, one very cool finish when he was one-on-one, rolling the ball into the corner, and then a penalty where he sent the goalkeeper the wrong way. At the other end, Jimmy was running the show from the half-back line, barking out instructions to keep everyone on their toes. Colm didn't say a word for the entire half, standing back from the line and writing down one or two notes.

'That was one of the best halves I've seen you play in

a long time,' he said when he brought us all together at the break. 'But,' he warned, 'it's only a half. These are a very, very good side, and if you give them even a tiny chance to get back into this, they'll take it. Go out there and finish the job now.'

Vincent's matched us score for score in the second half, but there was no drop in our performance. It was so impressive to watch. We were still five points ahead with 10 minutes to play when Colm told me to get ready to go on at full-back.

'We can't give them anything,' he told me. 'No easy points, no stupid frees. Nothing. Go in there and lock it down.'

'I will, don't worry.'

The next time the ball went dead, he sent me on. Jimmy had his hands on his knees, using the break in play to catch his breath. He had been everywhere, playing a blinder, and now he was exhausted.

'Ten more minutes,' I encouraged him as I ran past him to get into position. 'Let's finish it off.'

I was ready to walk into the middle of a war, but all of the big battles had already been won before I got there. We never gave them a chance. Even as we got tired, we weren't making many mistakes. We were still first to every ball; we were still there to stand in their way at every turn.

And when the referee blew the final whistle and we won by seven points, we were delighted – we had just earned a place in the Dublin Féile final, after all – but the celebrations weren't quite as exciting as I had imagined they would be. It felt like we were waiting for something.

Because winning a semi-final was never what this team was aiming for; we all knew that we still had one more job left to do.

'Enjoy these next two weeks.' Colm beamed as he shook every hand and patted us on the back afterwards. 'You only get one shot at Féile, and you've earned the right to be in the final. We'll be ready for whoever we come up against.

'Actually,' he said, 'I didn't want to do this until after the match. Before you go, there's something that I need to tell you.'

25

None of us could believe what we had just heard. It took a second for Colm's news to start to sink in.

'Sorry, Colm,' Jimmy interrupted, trying to make sure that we hadn't misunderstood. 'Are you saying –?'

'Yep,' Colm said, and the smile on his face told us he was deadly serious. 'The county board sent a message out to the four semi-finalists this week, but I didn't want to tell you before today's match. I didn't want you thinking about it. There was enough at stake already.

'So,' he asked, 'what do you think: are you ready to play in Croke Park?'

I was bouncing. It was all I could think about for the rest of the day. I had only been to Croke Park once or twice before, when Dad had somehow managed to get tickets for me, him and John to go to a Dublin match. I could still remember every detail of those days: the stadium drawing the crowds towards it; the fear that I might get split up from Dad and John and they would have to go in without me; the colour, the noise, the energy. It was more than just a stadium: there was something special about Croke Park.

At dinner, it was all that I wanted to talk about. We were going to play our Féile final in Ireland's biggest, most famous stadium. That night, I could barely sleep but I didn't mind. I lay there awake, imagining what it would be like to stand in the tunnel and run out onto that pitch and play. I couldn't wait for John to call so I could tell him.

There was a two-week break until the final, but it wasn't until training the following Tuesday evening that we found out who we would be playing against: St Christopher's. They had beaten Kilmacud Crokes by two points in the other semi-final.

'What was the match like?' I asked Colm. They had played on Sunday, the day after our game, so Colm had gone to watch it.

'Very good, very high quality, but that's what I expected so there were no real surprises. We know that Christopher's are a good team,' he said.

Even though they were the tougher opponent of the two, I was delighted we were playing Christopher's. I thought back to last year's league final and how much it had hurt to lose to them. Beating them in the league earlier this season hadn't made up for it, but beating them in the Féile final would. And – even though I knew I shouldn't be thinking this way – after what had happened in the Dublin academy, I couldn't wait to mark Andrew Devanney again.

'It'll be the same as before,' Colm said. 'It will be very tight, but if we play to our best, and they play to their best, there'll only be one winner.'

He had another surprise for us on Thursday: he had arranged for us to train up in Pairc Ciceam, the club's main pitch, where he and the rest of the senior team played all of their matches. We were usually allowed to use the pitch once a year, as a treat, for one of our matches towards the end of the season, but never for training.

'This pitch is unreal,' Kev said to me as an aeroplane flew in over our heads to land. From outside on the main road, we could see through the fence into Dublin Airport where all the planes were parked on the tarmac, ready to load up and take off.

'I know,' I said, admiring the grass. 'It's like someone was on their hands and knees cutting it with a scissors.'

'A scissors?' Jimmy said. 'You'd want to see if they'll do your next haircut for you, Philly, get away from that other barber of yours,' and everyone burst out laughing. I stuck my foot out and clipped his heels so that he stumbled, which set off another round of messing and jeering.

'This is one of the best pitches in the county,' Colm told us, trying to keep a lid on things. 'It won't be long now before you lads are on the senior team and you'll be training and playing up here all the time.'

Afterwards, he brought us into the clubhouse, and we packed into the senior team's dressing room. It was spotless, the walls painted white and the steel hooks empty, waiting for someone to come and hang a red and green jersey on each one. I sat down while a few of the others went poking around, running their hands over the wooden benches, investigating everywhere in case they might miss something.

'Which spot is yours?' Taz asked.

Colm pointed over to the corner. 'I try to take that one there most weeks.'

'Is that because it's closest to the physio table?' Taz asked, which made everyone laugh, Colm included.

'It's the quiet corner,' Colm explained. 'Well, the quietest corner – there's not really much quiet here on a match day. The lads at the other end like to play a bit of music, and some others have their headphones in, but I just like to sit there for a few minutes and think about the game before I start to get ready.

'Come here,' he said, 'I want to show you all something.'

We followed him back outside into the corridor, past the trophy cabinet and the framed Dublin jersey that hung on the wall, signed with a black marker just underneath where Colm's number three was printed. He stopped in front of a part of the wall that was blank except for one photo and waited for the rest of us to gather around.

'Do any of you know what this photo is?' he asked, tapping the edge of the frame with his finger. I was standing close enough that I could read the caption printed underneath it: Ballymun Kickhams – Dublin Féile Champions.

'That team won their Féile,' I said.

'Correct,' Colm said. 'There's nothing wrong with your eyesight anyway. But do you see how there's only one photo hanging up there?' He ran his hand over the blank wall. 'That's the last time a Ballymun Kickhams team won a Dublin Féile. That's the only time a Ballymun Kickhams team won a Dublin Féile.'

I hadn't realised that the club had only ever won one Féile in its history and, judging by the silence in the corridor, neither had anyone else. I understood now why Colm had brought us up to train here.

'This club has been waiting for twenty years to put another photo on the wall beside it. It's your turn now, lads.'

I took a close look at the faces in the photograph to see if I could recognise any of the players. Nobody seemed familiar, and there was no date on the photo, but as we walked away, I thought again about what Colm had said: *This club has been waiting for twenty years ...*

'Was that your Féile team?' I said to him quietly as we got outside. Everyone else was still studying the photo, imagining what it would be like to have one of our own hanging beside it in a few weeks' time.

'It was,' he said, and I could see that it still made him sad to talk about it. 'I had that row with the coach and went off to play soccer, and my team went and won Féile without me. I've been very lucky, I've won lots of medals, but I don't have one from Féile.'

'Not yet,' I said, and Colm seemed confused. 'The winning coach gets a medal too, right?' I asked.

'Yeah, they do.'

'We'll get you your medal next week,' I said. 'Sorry to keep you waiting so long for it.'

—

Something strange started to happen over the next few days. It started with one flag flying from the window of a house up in Balbutcher, and a hand-written sign stuck to the inside of the window of Macari's chipper. Mam pointed it out to me as we walked by. 'Look at that – that's very nice, isn't it?'

'*Best of luck to Ballymun Kickhams in the Féile final,*' I read. '*Bring home the cup!* How did they even know we were playing?' I asked Mam, who just shrugged her shoulders.

As we got into the week of the match, and closer to the day of the final, I noticed it more and more until, suddenly, it was hard to avoid. It wasn't just one flag in one house or one sign in Macari's; it was everywhere, an explosion of red and green. Bunting was hanging from every lamppost on both sides of the main road and all through Sillogue and Shangan and Balcurris and Balbutcher. Some of the lampposts had been sprayed in the Ballymun colours too.

It was only when I bumped into Mr O'Dea on his way home from the shops that I figured out what had happened.

'Philly – the very man,' he said, clapping me on the back with his free hand. He was delighted to see me. We chatted for a moment before he very gently asked about John. 'We're thinking about him all the time. Is he getting on okay over in London?'

I wasn't sure how much the neighbours knew about what was going on, or if they knew anything, but I liked Mr O'Dea, and I knew he wasn't being nosy. He genuinely cared. 'He's doing well, thanks. I'm hoping that he might be able to come home for our match this weekend.'

Mr O'Dea smiled at the good news. 'Well, I hope he's getting the best of care over there and that he'll be home soon. You tell him we were asking for him, won't you?'

'I will.'

'And tell me now, how are the preparations going for Sunday?' he said, the excitement creeping into his voice.

'Great, thanks. We've one more training session to-morrow but then that's it. I can't wait.'

'I know exactly how you're feeling. Rita and I will be there to cheer you on anyway – we wouldn't miss it.' He looked around at the disco of flags and bunting, dancing as the breeze picked up slightly. 'Isn't it wonderful to see all of the support and the club colours everywhere?'

'It's amazing. Where did it all come from, though?'

'Oh,' he chuckled, 'I may be partly responsible for that. I'm still on the residents' committee – I never managed to escape them after all these years – but when you won the semi-final, and when I heard the final was going to be in Croke Park, I thought this was something the whole community should get behind.'

'You made this happen?' I said, my eyes opening wide.

'Well, I thought we needed a bit of good news in the area, especially after that terrible story about what happened to your friends a few weeks ago.'

There had been reports about Al and Shane in the newspapers after the night they were attacked, although it didn't mention them by name because they were only teenagers. I didn't say that there very nearly could have been a third person caught up in it all that night.

'I just suggested that we should get some flags and banners printed up in the club colours and decorate the place, and that we should put a note in everyone's door to let them know when the final is being played and encourage them to show their support for the team.'

'That's amazing,' I said. 'Thank you.'

'Don't be silly,' he said. 'It's a big day for Ballymun. You and your teammates are out there representing our community. It's us who should be thanking you.'

I started to feel a bit emotional listening to Mr O'Dea, in his seventies now, telling me how much it would mean to him to see an Under-14 team run out into Croke Park in the Ballymun colours and play in the Féile final.

'I hope we can do it for you and make you proud on Sunday,' I said.

'You already have made us proud, Philly,' he said as he picked up his shopping bag to go home. 'Every single one of you. You already have. See you on Sunday.'

—

When I went home a while later, Mam was making pasta for dinner. 'It'll give you lots of good energy on Sunday,' she said. 'Croke Park is a big pitch.'

I sat up on the counter while she scraped the last few bits off the chopping board into the pan and boiled the kettle for the spaghetti. I told her about Mr O'Dea and the flags and the bunting, and Mam started to list off all of the people who had promised her they would be there on Sunday: family, friends, neighbours. She named practically everyone I had ever met – and plenty of people that I hadn't too – everyone except for one person.

So when John phoned home later that evening after dinner and I finally had a chance to speak to him, I asked him myself. It wouldn't be the same without having him there too.

I hadn't spoken to him since he'd left. He was only able to call a couple of evenings a week, and every time he phoned, I was out at training or somewhere else. On the nights when I stayed in hoping that he would call again, he never did.

When the phone rang, I raced to pick it up and I didn't let it go. I had so much to tell him about: the semi-final, Croke Park, the photograph in the clubhouse, the buzz all around Ballymun.

'They sprayed the lampposts and all for you?' He laughed. 'I hope they didn't paint over any of my graffiti. They're artworks at this stage – they've been there for years. How many people do you think will be there on Sunday?'

'I'm not sure. Judging by Mam's list, it sounds like it might be a sell-out.'

'It sounds absolutely amazing. I'm so proud of you, I really am. I wish I could be there with you all.'

'Is there any chance you could come home for a few days?' I asked. 'Even if you got the boat home on Saturday and then you went back first thing on Monday morning, that would be great. Just as long as you're here for the match.'

John sighed into the other end of the phone. 'I'd love to, I would. Do you know, no word of a lie, I was thinking the exact same thing myself – about getting the boat and just coming home for the weekend – and I even went and asked my doctor what she thought, but she told me it's not a good idea. She says I can't really take a break in my treatment at this point.'

'Don't worry, it's okay,' I said. I was upset that he

wouldn't be home, but there was no point in arguing with the doctor's advice. 'There'll be lots of other big matches in the future.'

'She's really good, the doctor,' John said. 'She says I've been doing great so far with the treatment. She thinks I'll probably only need another three or four weeks over here, and then I'll be able to come home for good.'

'Really?'

'Yeah. I know, I can't believe it either.' He sounded excited.

'How are you feeling?' I asked.

'Good,' he said. 'Really good.' He paused. 'I wasn't sure if I'd ever feel like this, but I think everything's going to be all right.'

Hearing him say that made me happier than anything. 'Of course it will,' I said. 'I know you can do it.'

'Listen, Philly, I'm going to have to go. My phone's beeping to tell me my money's about to run out. Tell Mam and Dad and Kellie I'm sorry I didn't get a chance to speak to them. I'll top the phone up tomorrow and chat to them soon.'

'I will. I'll see you in a few weeks,' I said. 'Love you.'

'Love you too, bro. I don't even need to wish you good luck for Sunday. I'm so proud of you.'

'I'm proud of you too,' I said, and then I heard the engaged tone. He was gone.

26

I wore my Kickhams tracksuit every day for the rest of the week, even though Mam had washed it and I knew I should have been keeping it clean for Sunday. As it got closer to the weekend, more and more people started to recognise the crest and the colours and wish me luck.

A woman pushing a buggy stopped me and Kev when we were on our way to training on Thursday. 'Are you on that football team that's in the final?' she asked me.

'Yeah, we both are,' I said.

'I heard them talking about you when I was in the shops earlier. I hope you win,' she said, taking her hand off the handle of the buggy to give us a thumbs up. 'Go on the Ballymun!'

Kev called over after dinner on Saturday night and the two of us sat outside on the landing and cleaned our boots together.

'Do you think we'll even be able to hear each other on the pitch?' Kev wondered, dipping a sponge into the green bucket and running it along the side of his boot again.

'I don't know,' I said. 'When they're doing interviews, the Dublin players always say they love hearing the noise of the fans, but it must just be there in the background. I'd say you block it out a bit when you're actually playing.'

Kev seemed happy with that answer, even though I was only guessing. It was my turn to start daydreaming a bit. 'I wonder where they'll do the trophy presentation. Will it be up in the Hogan Stand like they do for the All-Ireland?'

'That'd be deadly,' Kev said, and I suspected that, for a second, we were both imagining the exact same thing.

We walked around to the shops together on Sunday morning to meet the rest of the team. The minibus was already there waiting for us, the driver sitting in the front seat reading his newspaper, but other than that, we were the first two to arrive. When Taz showed up, he was messing around as usual, joking and trying to make people laugh, but everybody else was quieter than usual. They were definitely nervous, and that made me nervous.

It was only a short drive to Croke Park, less than ten minutes, and when it finally appeared out the window, it seemed even bigger, even more impressive than I remembered it. The minibus driver waited for the security guard to check our name off his list, slide open the gate for us and wave us through, and then he drove into the entrance underneath the stand before coming to a stop outside a set of double doors. The doors were closed but I could read the sign through the window – Dressing Rooms – and underneath it, a picture of the Ballymun Kickhams club crest.

'Lads, just hang on there for a couple of minutes,' Colm said as he got off the bus. 'I'll be back in five and we'll all go in together then.'

There was barely a word out of anyone while we waited for Colm to come back. When he brought us into the dressing room, a red and green jersey was hanging on every hook, the numbers on the backs facing outwards so we could see them.

'Sit anywhere you like for a minute,' Colm told us. 'I'll name the team now shortly and you can swap places then if you like.'

I put my gear bag down underneath the number 19, the same number I had worn in the semi-final. I had been training really well since then, but I still didn't know if I had done enough to start, and I didn't want Colm or anyone else to think that I was presuming I would. I took the jersey down from its hook to have a closer look at it. They weren't the jerseys that we normally wore – they were brand new. And as I turned it over, I saw that it had been embroidered on the front with the words 'Féile na nGael' under the crest.

There was still more than an hour to go before throw-in so we walked out to take a look at the pitch. One match had just finished, and another was about to start. There were so many clubs, so many teams, that we had all been divided up at the start of the tournament, but we were in Division A, the top division, which meant that our match would be the last one.

From where I was standing by the corner flag, the pitch looked enormous. I reached down and picked a blade of grass to rub between my fingers – I couldn't believe that I was actually here, standing on the Croke Park pitch – and then I threw it up in the air and watched it float back to the ground. I had seen players on TV do that before, to see which way the wind was blowing, but there wasn't even a puff of breeze inside the ground. It was a beautiful day.

The stand was already a sea of red and green, the Ballymun fans and flags dominating all of the others.

As we made our way up along the sideline towards the halfway line, I spotted Mam and Dad and June and Lindy and Kellie. Mam and Dad were both wearing jerseys, and June and Lindy and Kellie had their faces painted, half in red, half in green. Kellie had made a poster too, and when she saw me looking up, she held it up so that I could read it: 'Philly's Gonna Get Ya,' it said.

'Look, there they are,' I said, pointing them out to Kev, and he looked up and waved. Trish, his mam, was sitting beside them. Mr and Mrs O'Dea were there too, a couple of rows in front of Mam and Dad; as I ran my eye further down along the same row, I saw the Flynns, our next-door neighbours.

'Did you know Michelle Flynn was going to be here?' I asked Kev.

'Yeah, I asked her,' he said, as if it was the most natural thing in the world.

'Seriously?' I didn't mean to sound quite so surprised. I had only ever heard Kev talk about Michelle Flynn, never actually talk to her.

'Yeah,' he said, and his face went a little red. 'I was hanging around with her and some of her friends there for a while earlier in the summer. They're all sound. You'd like them.'

'You kept that one quiet! I'm not gonna steal your girlfriend, like.'

'Shut up, she's not my girlfriend,' he said, going redder and redder. 'Well, maybe she is, I dunno. Anyway, I'll introduce you to her later.'

'Introduce me?' I tried not to fall over laughing. 'Kev, she's been my next-door neighbour for the last thirteen years, you mad yoke. I think I'll be all right without the introduction, thanks.'

He went to give me a dig as I burst out laughing again. Colm appeared just in time to save him from any further embarrassment

'How are you feeling?' he asked as he pulled me aside for a chat.

'Excited,' I said, and it was the truth.

'That's what I like to hear. You're starting at full-back.'

Part of me felt like I had been holding my breath all morning, waiting for Colm to make his decision. I was so relieved.

'You're going to have your hands full,' he said, giving me his instructions. 'Andrew Devanney is probably going to be in at full-forward and I want you marking him again today. If he's playing further out the field, you go with him, and I'll get one of the lads to drop in and cover you. But whatever you do, don't give him an inch.'

We went back into the dressing room so Colm could announce the team. I didn't even hear him call out my name. I was lost in concentration, checking everything twice – my jersey, shorts, socks, gloves, boots – to make sure they were perfect, and then checking them again. Boots *clack-clack*ed on the ground as lads started to move around, the energy slowing rising in the room. Colm made us sit down again before we went out, but his team-talk was short.

'You deserve to be here, lads. You've prepared perfectly. You've trained hard,' he reminded us. 'We play football because we enjoy it, so go out there and enjoy yourselves. If you do that, the rest will take care of itself.'

He looked over to me. 'As captain, anything you'd like to add before we go out?'

'I just hope someone has brought a camera,' I shouted as I stood up, 'because we're not leaving here without a photo for that wall. Let's go, Ballymun!'

—

It was nearly half-time before I had an opportunity to catch my breath again. From the moment the ball was thrown in, everything happened at triple speed, and if you stopped for a second, you'd be left behind. It felt more like a fight up at the Monos after school, except every punch was landing and nobody was backing down.

We scored.

They scored.

They scored.

We scored.

The Croke Park pitch was every bit as big as it looked, and by half-time, I knew every inch of it. Andrew Devanney never stopped running. More than once, he dropped all the way back into his own half-back line, and I went with him, which made me wonder if he'd been told to just move me around the pitch, drag me out of position, and hope that it would it leave a few gaps for his teammates close to our goal. If that was their plan, it was working for them. He didn't score from play in the first half, but their other forwards were getting enough space to make chances and take them. All I could do was look on from a distance.

'I don't even know where he's playing,' I said to Colm at half-time. Christopher's had started to get on top as the half went on, and we were losing by three points. 'Are you sure you want me to keep following him around the place?'

'How many points has he kicked?' Colm asked.

'Just those two frees,' I said as I took another drink from my water bottle.

'Then you're doing your job, and you're doing it well. Keep doing it. We're still in this.'

But we were being overrun. It felt like we were hanging on by a thread and that every chance Christopher's had was a chance to kill the game off. They got through on goal twice early in the second half, and twice Martin made big saves to stop them. The attacks kept coming in waves and every tackle was more and more desperate, more and more last-ditch.

If it wasn't for Taz, we would have been dead and buried. While we were scrambling to plug holes at the back, he was having the game of his life at the other end. He kicked three points in a row – two off his right and one off his left – and as the last of the three sailed between the posts and the Ballymun flags started waving with a little bit more belief, Colm called me back over to the sideline. Christopher's lead was back down to two again, but we were running out of time.

'There's only three or four minutes left here,' he told me. 'We'll get the chances, but we need to stop them from scoring again. No easy points, no stupid frees. Nothing.'

I sprinted back into position and Christopher's were on the attack again. Colm was right; another point and they'd nearly be out of reach. Their corner-forward got around Seán, our corner-back. We were caught short and the whole pitch opened up for him. I was expecting him to bring it in towards goal to make a better angle for himself or maybe wait for some support to try and turn it into a goal chance. That would really kill the game.

But he took the shot on early. I was standing under the posts, watching, waiting in case it dropped, willing it to go wide. And it did.

'What's left, ref?' Kev asked as we got back into position, but before he got an answer, Martin had taken the kickout quickly. Jimmy had peeled out towards the sideline, where nobody was marking him, and Martin hit him on the run with an inch-perfect kick.

The Christopher's lads were out of position, scrambling to get back behind the ball. Taz had drifted inside and was one-on-one with his marker. Jimmy looked up when he heard him roar and saw his hand in the air. From the halfway line, he launched the ball goalwards, hoping that Taz would be able to wriggle away from his marker to win it.

The two of them grappled and wrestled while the ball came towards them. Colm was roaring from one dugout for a free in; the Christopher's manager was roaring from the other for a free out. But the referee kept his whistle in his hand while the ball dropped. Taz got out in front of his marker and reached for it with both hands. He got both of his gloves on it, and I knew he'd immediately be thinking of his quickest way towards goal. This was our chance. But as he landed and went to turn, a hand came through from behind and slapped the ball away before he could pull it in to his chest safely.

Time stood still for a moment as the ball broke, bobbling away from Taz and his marker. They both reacted instantly and scrambled towards it, but neither of them got there first.

Kev swooped in, running on from midfield, and burst on to the ball. There was nobody between him and the goal. He took one solo, one hop, and as the keeper raced out to him to close him down and narrow the angle, doing anything he could to smother the chance, Kev put his head down and struck the ball straight through his laces.

From where I was standing, I couldn't see the net ripple, but I could hear the roar from the Ballymun crowd, and then I saw Kev running back towards midfield, high-fiving and punching the air. A goal. We had gone from two points down to one point ahead, and there couldn't be more than a minute or two left to play. I wanted to run and celebrate with Kev but there was no time. It would have to wait. We couldn't let this slip away from us now.

Christopher's came at us again. They knew this would probably be their last chance, and I knew they would try to get the ball to one player. Andrew Devanney pushed off me and ran out into space, screaming for the ball. I went with him. I had to be careful. I knew that a free was as good as a score to him, and if I gave him that chance, he wouldn't miss.

He got his hands on the ball and turned, and now I was on the back foot. He could see the posts, the whole pitch opening up in front of him, and I was blind. It was just the two of us, one-on-one.

I waited for him to move back onto his right foot, his strong foot, the foot that he'd want to shoot off. But he didn't. He shaped to shoot with his left, which caught me by surprise and nearly threw me off balance. That was his plan. As I stumbled, he shifted his weight, and now I was out of the picture. He had a clear sight on goal. He took one last look at the posts to pick his spot and then took the shot.

I was too far away to try to make a tackle. There wasn't time to do anything else. I threw myself across his path, both arms outstretched, and hoped. The ball cannoned off the palms of my hands and when I lifted my head and looked up, it was rolling away towards the sideline. I had blocked it.

Jimmy scooped up the loose ball with his boot and tried to blast it all the way back to Ballymun; the further, the better. The referee had blown the final whistle before it landed again. It was all over. We were the champions of Dublin.

From that moment on, everything was a blur. I lay where I was on the ground, listening to the cheers from the stand. I wanted to run, to see Mam and Dad and everyone else to give them a hug and to celebrate, but I was too tired to move. That was my first mistake, as Kev, Taz, Jimmy, Martin, Liam and the rest of the team piled on top of me in celebration. Through the bodies, I could hear Kev leading the chant up on the top:

'Go on, go on, go on the Ballymun.

Go on, go on, go on the Ballymun.'

When I dragged myself out of the bottom of the pile and finally got back to my feet, I grabbed him for a hug and let out a roar that was nothing but happiness.

'We did it,' I said, grabbing his face between my hands. 'We did it.'

I didn't know where to turn next. I wanted to see everyone, celebrate with everyone. Where was Colm? Before I could go to look for him, there was a tap on my shoulder, and Andrew Devanney was standing there. His eyes were red, and it looked like he had been crying.

'Good game,' he said with a bit of a sniff, holding out his hand towards me. 'You're a great team.'

I reached out and shook his hand.

'I'm sorry about what happened before,' he apologised. 'I didn't mean what I said. I shouldn't have said it.'

'And I'm sorry for giving you a smack,' I said, 'so I think it's fair to call it quits.'

He smiled at that. 'Enjoy the celebrations. I'd say Gerry was impressed with you today,' he added as he turned to leave. 'Hopefully see you back in the academy soon.'

The academy – I had completely forgotten that Gerry Mangan would be there to watch us. As I ran towards the Hogan Stand, I spotted him over on the sideline, talking to Colm. Whether it was good news or bad, it could wait. Mam had run down from her seat to the front of the stand, shouting and waving to try and get my attention. 'Philip! Philip!'

I jumped up onto the barrier to give her a hug before she climbed over it and ran onto the pitch herself to get to me.

'I'm so proud of you,' she said and she was crying too, except hers were tears of happiness. 'I love you.'

'Love you too, Mam. Thanks for everything.'

I could have stayed there for the rest of the day celebrating, but I only had time to give Dad and my sisters a quick hug before Kev pulled me away. 'Come on, you've to go. They're waiting for you.'

'Waiting for what?' I hadn't a clue what he was talking about.

'You've to go up and get the trophy first before they do the medal presentation. They've been calling your name and everything.'

'Oh right, yeah, okay.' I had completely forgotten. 'Come on so,' I said, pushing him in front of me. 'You're coming too.'

'I can't,' Kev protested. 'It's only the captain for the trophy. I'll wait and go up with the rest of the team.'

I ignored him and kept pushing him ahead of me towards the steps. 'Captains,' I insisted. 'I wouldn't even be playing today except that you convinced me to come back. We're both the captains. We're both going up to get this trophy together.'

Kev stopped and looked me in the eye, trying to figure out if this was a wind-up. When he saw that I was deadly serious, he took off in a sprint towards the presentation area, leaving me to chase after him. We raced up the steps, taking them two at a time, to collect our medals. The chairman of the Dublin county board was there to make the presentation, and after he said a few words, he asked if either of the captains would like to make a speech. I winked at Kev as I took the microphone out of the chairman's hand.

'This is a very short speech,' I said. 'It's only three words long, really … YUP THE FLATS!' I roared.

With our medals swinging from our necks, we took a handle of the trophy each and lifted it. A stampede broke out behind us as the rest of the lads charged up the steps to get their hands on it and take their turn at lifting it. There was a bit of fuss as the lads sorted themselves out into an orderly queue, and when the chairman's back was turned, I slipped a second medal off the tray and went back down onto the pitch.

Colm was standing there by himself, watching the celebrations as the lads kissed their medals – Taz took a bite of his to make sure it was real – and then took it in turns to either put the lid of the cup on their heads or to pretend to drink out of it.

'This one's for you,' I said to Colm as I pressed it into the palm of his hand. 'I hope you haven't run out of room for it after all these years.'

'Thank you, Philly,' he said. I watched him fold the ribbon up neatly and then put it into his pocket. 'I really appreciate that. You were super out there again today. I don't know how you kept going. And that block at the end … I don't know how you managed that.'

'I don't know either,' I admitted.

'I have another bit of news for you too,' Colm said. 'Gerry Mangan said to pass on his best wishes and his congratulations. Actually, I think what he said was, "I know there's no man of the match award in Féile, but they should have made one for the number three."'

'That's very nice of him. I think I'd have picked Taz myself,' I said.

Colm smiled. 'It's funny you should say that. Taz was the other player he mentioned. He asked me to tell you both that the next academy training session is in three weeks' time, and he's looking forward to seeing you both there.'

'Are you serious? Did he say anything about the fight?'

'It's all forgotten,' Colm said. 'You didn't make it easy for yourself, but you've definitely earned it. This is only the beginning, though, so make the most of it.'

'I will. Thanks, Colm.'

'Now go on and tell your mam and dad,' he said. 'They'll be delighted.'

They were – but there was one person who I knew would be the most delighted of all, and I couldn't wait to tell him.

'Can I've a look at your phone there quickly, please, Dad? I just want to give John a ring. He'll be raging that he's missed all of this.'

Dad passed me his phone and I scrolled down until I found John's English number and pressed Dial. It was noisy over by the stands, so I held the phone tight to my ear and walked into the middle of the pitch to try to hear it better, but all I could hear was the ringtone. John wasn't answering. I waited a few minutes, in case he hadn't heard it ring the first time, and tried him again. Still no answer; he must have been either out or busy. I handed Dad back his phone. I'd try him again later.

After the celebrations had finally simmered down and we had got clean and changed, we all went back to the Kickhams clubhouse for a party. By the time we got there, the place was jammed. People were outside chatting and drinking, and inside, it was nearly impossible to move. It felt like all of Ballymun must have been there.

It was late by the time we got home again, and I decided to try John one more time before I went to bed. This time, the phone only rang for a few seconds before it was answered, but the voice on the end belonged to a man I didn't recognise.

'Hello? John?' I said.

'This is John's phone,' the man said. He was very polite with a posh English accent. 'Who am I speaking to?'

'Tell him it's Philly, his brother. I just wanted to chat to him for a minute before I go to bed.'

The man didn't respond for a few moments and I wondered if I had been cut off.

'Can I ask if John's parents are near you at the moment?' he said gently. 'And if so, could I speak to one of them, please?'

'Stop messing, will you? Just put John on there, please. Tell him we won our match. I'll only be a second.'

'If I could speak to either of your parents, please, that would be great,' he said, persisting. 'This is Sergeant Richard Taylor of the London Metropolitan Police speaking. I'm afraid I have some bad news.'

27

I don't know if I'll ever forget the look on Mam's face as she sat there silently, listening to what Sergeant Taylor had to say. She didn't cry at first, or shout or scream. She didn't do any of the things that I expected someone to do when they've been told that a line has been drawn through their life, that there's now a before and an after, and that their world will never be the same again. Her face was blank, giving no sign of the terrible news she was trying to process. It was as if someone had flicked a switch and her light had gone out.

But the moment she hung up the phone, her tears turned from a trickle to a stream to a river in an instant.

'What happened?' I asked, although I didn't want her to answer. 'Is John okay?'

She shook her head. She couldn't bring herself to say it.

'What did the police say? Where is he?'

Mam forced the words out. 'They found him in his room this morning, but it was already too late. They couldn't wake him up.'

Dad sat down on one side of her and squeezed her hand, and Kellie sat on the other.

'What do you mean they couldn't wake him up?' I needed to hear her say it. I wouldn't believe it was true until she did.

'He died in his sleep last night,' she whispered. 'Oh, John, I'm sorry. I'm so, so sorry. We left you over there all alone …'

I didn't understand. Mam must have misheard or the policeman must have gotten mixed up. It didn't make sense. There was a taste of metal in my mouth and I tried to swallow it away. I thought I was going to throw up. 'No. There must be some mistake. Call them back. How do they know it's John? It could be someone else. He's getting better. He told me the other day. His doctor said he'd be ready to come home again in a few more weeks.'

She shook her head. 'There's no mistake. It's okay. It'll be okay.' She turned to face me as she spoke but she wasn't looking at me. She wasn't looking at anything.

Thoughts ran through my head at a million miles an hour. I couldn't think straight. He'd told me that he was off drugs, that he was on his rehab programme. He was so close to being better, for good. I thought of him lying there after one hit too many, with nobody there to help him. I needed to know that what he'd told me was true, and that he hadn't died of an overdose.

'How, though? How did he just die in his sleep?'

'I don't know. They won't know that for a few days. They'll have to do a post-mortem on him.'

'But where was he when they found him? What had he been doing?'

Mam finally understood what I meant. 'No, no, it's not like that. The sergeant on the phone said that they knew he was in his treatment programme, but there was no sign that he had been using drugs again, nothing like that. The doctor said he was reasonably certain that he had a heart attack while he was asleep. It will just take a few days to know for sure.'

That made even less sense. Heart attacks weren't supposed to happen to young men who hadn't even turned twenty yet. None of this was supposed to happen. He was supposed to get better. He was supposed to come home. We were supposed to be a family again.

Mam asked me to come and sit with them on the couch but I couldn't sit. I didn't know where to go, so I went out into the hall. A picture of the two of us sitting outside the flats with Dad, after playing football, was hanging on the wall. I just wanted to look at it so I could see John's face again. I already felt like I was starting to forget what he looked like. I walked by that photo so many times every day, invisible on the wall, and I hardly ever stopped to look at it; now it was all that I had left.

The tears stung my eyes again. I went into our bedroom and lay down on the bed. I buried my face deep into my pillow and I roared. I roared as loud as I could, to get it all out of me. I thought it might help me feel better but it didn't. Nothing could.

It seemed like hardly anything was left in our bedroom that reminded me of John, apart from one or two of his old music posters, peeling away at the corners where the Blu Tack was coming loose. Most of the stuff in our room was mine; John never really had much, and most of what he did have, he had fit into a couple of small bags and taken to London with him.

I went over to the wardrobe and reached into the back of it. I knew what I was looking for and that it was in there somewhere. It didn't take me long to find the paper bag and, inside it, the Dublin jersey still sealed in its plastic wrap, the tags still on it, untouched since the day John had given it to me.

I sat back down on the side of the bed and opened it. I didn't put it on. I just held it in my hands. The teardrops landed on it in circles and turned the crisp sky blue into blotches of a darker shade. I didn't bother trying to stop them. I didn't care.

—

On my birthday, two days later, I flew to London with Mam and June and Kellie so we could bring John home.

All we had was a piece of paper with the address of the hostel that John had been staying in while attending the treatment centre. When the four of us turned onto the street where his hostel was, I could see why he might not have mentioned it to any of us, not even to Mam and Dad. It was a beautiful afternoon and the sun was shining, but this felt like a forgotten part of the city. I imagined that London would be this colourful place, full of energy, but the only colours here were black and white and grey. Where there used to be shops and homes, now there were just boarded-up buildings and smashed windows. The only sign that anybody still came here was the frames of the stalls lining both sides of the road, but everyone had gone home now, and it looked like a ghost market or something out of a zombie film.

John's hostel was at the opposite end of the road, a small door with no sign on it tucked away between a closed-down butcher's and a shop that repaired old record players. Something about the place felt wrong to me, even before we had squeezed our way up the narrow staircase, one after the other. It looked like a place that was trying too hard to be clean and tidy and not quite able to manage it. The walls were supposed to be white but they had turned a disgusting pale yellow, covered in dirt and other strange marks. All of the doors in the building were steel, even the bedroom doors, and the paint had chipped away from them in places. They made the place feel more like a prison than a home.

Sergeant Taylor met us at the reception and walked us down to John's bedroom. It was empty and bare, except for two little boxes that the hostel staff had used to pack away John's things. Even though it was tiny, not even as big as the room we shared, it didn't seem like John had enough stuff to fill it and make it feel like home. There was a mattress on a steel frame in one corner, and a small boxy television in another, and that was it. A wave of a smell hit me all of a sudden, like the Jeyes Fluid disinfectant that Mam used to clean the landing outside the flat and sometimes poured down into the stairwells. Everything about the place made me feel sick.

I pushed past June and Kellie and ran back down the stairs. I made it just in time – when the air from outside hit my face, I threw up on the side of the road.

When I went back upstairs, Mam was at reception filling out some forms while June and Kellie sat and waited on two hard plastic chairs, the same as the ones we had in school. The two boxes with John's belongings were at their feet.

'How are you doing?' Sergeant Taylor asked me when I reappeared.

'I'm okay,' I said, which was half-true. I wasn't going to be sick again – at least I didn't think so – but I'm sure he could tell from one look at me that I was anything but okay. I had thought about Sergeant Taylor a lot since his phone call, and he was nearly exactly how I'd pictured him: tall with neat, dark hair, and not as much as a crease or a spot to be found on his black uniform. He looked like the kind of person who did a lot of running to keep fit; I wouldn't fancy getting a chase from him, but he was on our side, and it was reassuring to have him there with us.

He took an envelope from inside his jacket and handed it to me. 'This is for you,' he said. 'The staff found it on John's bedside locker but he never got a chance to send it before …' He stopped, and started again. 'I wanted to make sure that you got it,' he explained.

My name and our address were written on the front, and there was a stamp with a picture of the Queen of England stuck in the top right-hand corner. I turned it over to open it, but the back of the envelope was already unstuck.

'We had to check it to see what it was,' Sergeant Taylor apologised, and then he added, 'I hope you don't mind me saying this but he really loved you.'

I smiled and I nodded and tried not to cry again. 'I know. Thanks.'

Mam finished filling out the forms and asked if we were ready to leave. She was already tired and we still had a lot left to do. I couldn't wait to get out of that horrible hostel and never ever see it again.

The others walked on ahead of me and got into the police car while I stopped outside and opened the envelope that Sergeant Taylor had given me. Inside was a birthday card and, tucked into the middle, folded neatly on little sheets of writing paper, was one last letter from John to me.

28

I waited until our flight had taken off before I opened the envelope again and read John's letter for the first time.

I read it twice: quickly at first, rushing through to get to the end, and then more slowly the second time around, taking my time over every word. I could hear his voice in my head as I read it. We never had a chance to say goodbye, so this was it. It felt like he was there with me one last time, messing up my hair or digging me in the arm one minute and then reminding me how proud he was the next; telling me how excited he was to get better and come home so he could be right there beside me as I chased my dream.

And as I read it, I understood everything a little better. I was chasing that dream for both of us now.

Mam had her eyes closed in the seat beside me. I didn't want to disturb her. It had been a long few days for everyone, but for her in particular, and I knew she was exhausted. The captain came on the PA system to make an announcement about landing, and Mam opened her eyes and looked at me.

'Were you asleep?' I said.

'No, I was just thinking.'

I handed her the birthday card and the letter.

'Where did you get this?

'Sergeant Taylor gave it to me. It's from John.'

'He remembered your birthday,' she said, shaking her head.

'Yeah, he always did. That was why I got two presents every year,' I reminded her, 'one from you and Dad and the girls, and then a second one just from John. He'd always get me a new football or something, remember? Or that year when he came home with the hamster and you had to make him bring it back to the shop?'

We had wanted to call him Henrik after Henrik Larsson, the Celtic striker. I laughed at the memory of it, which made Mam smile too.

When she was finished reading, she folded the letter carefully and placed it back into the birthday card, then slipped the card back into the envelope. 'That's very special,' she said as she took hold of my hand and held it in hers on top of the armrest. 'Put it somewhere safe. You never let it out of your sight, do you hear me?'

'Is anybody going to speak at the funeral?' I asked. 'You know, to tell a story about John?'

'I'm sure someone will. I don't know. I haven't thought about it yet.'

'Could I do it? I think I'd like to.'

'Of course,' she said, giving my hand a little squeeze. 'I think he would have really liked that.'

It was night time when we got back to Ballymun. When we got to the front door, it was already open and there was a hum of voices inside. I had thought Dad would be by himself while we were away, or that he might have gone out to meet his friends if he didn't want to be at home alone, but when we went inside, six or seven of the neighbours were in the sitting room with him. Mr and Mrs O'Dea were sitting on the couch talking to Claire Mac from upstairs. Trish, Kev's mam, was in the kitchen with Mags Flynn from next door, boiling the kettle for another round of tea.

When I opened the fridge to get something to drink,

it was full to the edge of every shelf with lasagnes and shepherd's pies and big tubs of chicken curry and home-made cakes – enough to feed two families for a month.

Trish came over to give me a hug and saw me staring at the food. 'We wanted to make sure you had enough to do you for the next few days,' she said.

'Did you do this?' I asked.

'Everybody did a little bit,' she said. 'You know we'll always mind each other.'

'I know,' I said, even though I couldn't quite believe they had done all of this for us. 'Thank you.'

They stayed until it was late into the night and then left so we could try to get some sleep, but by the time I woke up again, there was a brand-new set of familiar faces, there to make tea and drink tea and sit and chat and just be with us. I took a few photos of John off the wall and I stood them up on the kitchen counter and in the sitting room. At least that way he could still be at the heart of it all, just the way he would have wanted it.

The night before the funeral, we brought John's coffin back to the flat so that he could spend one last night at home with us before he was buried. It was a strange feeling. Everyone who called up to visit us was so sad, but at the same time, they all had their own funny story or happy memory of how much John had meant to them, and I loved hearing all of them.

The next morning, I put on my shirt and trousers and brushed my jacket to make sure it was clean. When it was time, the priest came into the flat and said the prayers, and we stood by the coffin one last time with John. He looked like he was asleep. I wanted to say goodbye but I knew that I couldn't; it was too late.

We walked behind the hearse as it brought John around the blocks one last time, the place where he had spent so many hours, and then slowly made its way down the road to the church. It felt like all of Ballymun was standing there, waiting for us to arrive.

It wasn't until I stood up at the altar that I realised quite how many people were there. It was a big church and every single seat was taken, and then there were rows of people lining both sides of the church and all along the back as well, three or four deep in places. It took me a moment to gather my thoughts before I started to speak.

'Thank you all for coming this morning. This week has been the toughest one of our lives, and we couldn't have done it without you. I just wish that John could be here to see how much he meant to so many people. He'd want me to tell you that he loved you all – even the ones of you that he hated.'

I waited for everyone to stop laughing before I continued.

'I'm only messing. Anyone who ever met John knows that he didn't hate anybody. He was the kindest, most generous person, the man with the biggest heart. And that made me the luckiest person in the world, because he was my big brother.'

I could feel the tears coming but I was determined to keep going.

'I wish he was here so that I could tell him how much I loved him. Over the last few weeks, we talked about how much we were looking forward to him getting better so that we could stop worrying and spend our time doing all of the things that big brothers and their little brothers do together.

'He was so excited when I got called into the Dublin academy a few months ago. He was so excited when our team got to the Féile final last weekend. He kept telling me how excited he was to see what I was going to do next and to be right there beside me. I never got a chance to tell him that I felt the same way about his future too.'

I had a piece of paper in my hand with some notes that I had written down, but I put it back in my pocket and just said what was in my head.

'John was addicted to heroin, and I thought that needed to be kept a secret. I thought that our family should hide it away, that we should never talk about it.

I didn't even want people to know that I was related to him. I was so embarrassed by him that I even changed my surname. I thought that I was helping him by pushing him away, but I know now that it only made things worse. I'll never know how lonely that made him feel when he needed me the most.'

The words hung in the silence while I paused to think of what I wanted to say next. Every face in the church was staring back at me.

'I'm not embarrassed by you, John,' I continued. 'I'm proud of you, proud of everything that you went through and how you kept on fighting. I tried to tell you that the last night we spoke on the phone. I don't know if you even heard me.

'If you were still here, I know you'd tell everyone that there should be no more secrets. You would want to tell people about your life and all of the lessons you learned and the mistakes that you made. You wouldn't care if people judged you. All you'd care about is telling your story, because maybe that would help someone else. You can't do that now, but I can. I can tell your story for you. And I will.

'Sleep tight, John. Thanks for being the best big brother in the world. I love you.'

I used the cuff of my shirt to wipe my eyes as I walked back to my seat and sat in between Mam and Dad.

'That was perfect,' Dad said as he handed me a tissue. Mam just kissed me on the side of the head.

After the priest said the final prayers, I lifted John's coffin with Dad and some of my uncles and cousins. We walked slowly through the church as people bowed their heads. All of John's gang – Aaron, Ciarán, Trev, Joey – were standing together at the back of the church. Aaron forced a smile as he caught my eye, but the tears kept rolling down his cheeks. As we stepped outside, I saw the red and green of Ballymun Kickhams. All of my teammates were there, standing in two lines on either side, forming a guard of honour for John as we carried him to the hearse. We were all part of the same family; they were my brothers too.

At the graveyard, two men with shovels waited off to the side. As I walked over to the edge of the hole that they had dug and looked down into it, it started to rain.

The priest blessed John and then the men came over and lowered his coffin until it disappeared into the ground. Mam had a single flower in her hand. She kissed the top of it, then placed it into the grave, and Dad and June and Lindy and Kellie did the same. Everyone took one last moment to say goodbye and then, one by one, they stepped back and moved away.

And when everyone else had started to walk back down the path towards the main gates, and it was just me standing there alone by myself, I opened the paper bag in my hand and took out the Dublin jersey that John had bought for me.

'This one is yours,' I said as I let it fall out of my hand and in on top of John's coffin. 'I'll earn one for myself, and when I do, it will be for you too. I won't stop trying until I get one.

'I'll make you proud. I promise.'

TALKING POINTS

- Why do you think this book is called *The Choice*? Is it a good title?
- Why do good people sometimes make bad choices?
- What is the most important choice Philly makes in the book?
- If you had to give the book a different title, what would it be?
- What scene has stuck with you the most?
- Did you find this story a good read? If so, what kept you turning the pages?
- If you could ask the author a question, what would it be?

- Did this book remind you of any other books you have read, or TV programmes or films you have watched?
- This book reads like a novel, but it is based on real experiences. What difference does that make to how you read it?
- Philly is a member of several groups of people. Family. Friends. Community. Team. Which do you think is most important to him and why?
- Are there any details of Philly's life as he describes it that particularly surprised you?
- Which character in the book do you most admire? Why?
- Would you like to have John as a big brother? Why? Why not?
- How does Philly's relationship with John change in the course of the book?
- What does this book tell you about nature and nurture – whether people are born a certain way or are formed by how and where they are brought up?
- Did you learn anything from this book about the dangers of drugs that you didn't already know?
- What does this story tell you about courage? Who shows courage and when?
- This book was written by a famous sports person. What does it tell you about sport? What did sport mean to him?

- Lots of things that happen in the book don't seem fair. Do you think the characters in the book get what they deserve?
- Do you know what a stereotype is? In what way are stereotypes important in this book?
- Philly gets the chance to make up for some of his bad choices. Can you think of decisions you wish you had the chance to make again?
- What impression does the book give you of Ballymun – the good things as well as the bad?
- The book ends with a funeral. Is it a good ending? Did you find it upbeat or downbeat?